"You're too easy a target at home."

Jessica stared at him, dumbfounded that Andrew expected her to run and hide. "I won't be run out of my home by anyone."

"I'm only suggesting you take precautions. You've stayed at the shelter lots of times."

"By choice." She folded her arms. "You're suggesting I hide out."

"What's wrong with that?"

"I won't let one of these psychos control my life." She wouldn't allow that to happen again.

"Need I remind you that you were nearly killed yesterday?" he said. "This guy has already scared you half to death and all he did was get onto the porch and rattle the door. What are you going to do when he gets inside?"

"I was not scared."

He closed the distance between them as if his closeness was a reminder. "You were trembling. Are you so stubborn that you won't even admit when you're afraid?"

Not to him. But she admitted it to herself. She was terrified....

VIRGINIA VAUGHAN

was born and raised in Mississippi and has never strayed far beyond those borders. She feels blessed to come from a large Southern family, and her fondest memories include listening to stories recounted by family and friends around the large dinner table. She was a lover of books even from a young age, devouring gothic romance novels and stories of romance, danger and love. She soon started writing them herself.

After marriage, two kids and a divorce, Virginia realized her characters needed the same thing she needed—the healing grace and restoration power of Jesus Christ. She devoted her life and her writing to His glory and watched God swing open doors for her to walk through.

You can connect to Virginia through her website, virginiavaughanonline.com.

No Safe Haven

Virginia Vaughan

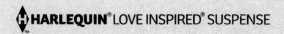
HARLEQUIN® LOVE INSPIRED® SUSPENSE

Recycling programs for this product may not exist in your area.

LOVE INSPIRED BOOKS

ISBN-13: 978-0-373-44617-9

NO SAFE HAVEN

Copyright © 2014 by Virginia Vaughan

This edition published by arrangement with Love Inspired Books.

® and TM are trademarks of Love Inspired Books, used under license. Trademarks indicated with ® are registered in the United States Patent and Trademark Office, the Canadian Intellectual Property Office and in other countries.

www.Harlequin.com

Printed in U.S.A.

I will repay you for the years the locusts have eaten—
the great locust and the young locust,
the other locusts and the locust swarm.
—*Joel* 2:25

To my Lord and Savior Jesus Christ
through whom all things are possible.

And to my writer's group, the Bards of Faith.
You've been there for me through both the tears
and the laughter. You have encouraged,
challenged and inspired me throughout this journey.
I love each and every one of you and
I am so thankful God brought you into my life.

ONE

The slam of a car door grabbed Jessica Taylor's attention.

She dropped the clothes in her hand and rushed to the window to scan the front of the house. An unfamiliar silver sedan was parked at the curb. That hadn't been there when Jessica arrived to help Sarah Young escape her abusive husband.

Sarah's face was pale against the blue bruises that shadowed her eye and cheeks and the red swollen lip. But it was the fear in her wide, green eyes that spoke volumes. "It's Robert. He's home," she said, her voice a choked, fearful whisper.

The thought of a confrontation with this man—or any man who believed he had the right to beat his wife—swept a wave of bitterly familiar emotions through Jessica. Fear, desperation, hopelessness. For a moment, she was swept back into the past to another confrontation.

The pounding on the door...the despair...the chilling voice on the other side of the door.

You're mine, Jess.

No matter how many times she'd confronted such evil, she'd never grown accustomed to it.

But she'd also learned to push through her fears until the singe of righteous anger strengthened her and she would never bow to them. She ignored the shakiness in her knees as she pulled her long blond hair into a pony-tail. She only wished she were more dressed down. High-heeled shoes were not the ideal for running if she needed to, but she'd come straight from court and she liked the added height they gave her five-foot-six frame.

She draped on an air of calmness as she turned to Sarah. "Grab your suitcase. We need to go now. He won't find you. You'll be safe, I promise."

Sarah's chin quivered and tears pooled in her eyes. "He's going to be so mad."

Jessica knew this was a pivotal moment. The attack on Sarah was damaging enough to keep her husband in jail overnight, but they'd lost precious escape time while she'd tried to convince Sarah to leave. Even now, she saw the question of whether or not to go on Sarah's battered face.

Jessica understood her feelings. This was Sarah's home and she didn't want to leave it, but she also knew the statistics of intimate partner violence. Robert's vio-lence was escalating, and Sarah might not survive an-other attack.

Jessica touched her arm, trying to pull the young woman's focus back to the plan. "Sarah, we have to leave. Robert doesn't know about Dean's Den. You'll be safe there, but we have to go now."

The domestic violence shelter Jessica ran in Jackson had safeguards for women in Sarah's position. But those security measures would be futile if Robert had an op-portunity to follow them there.

Sarah nodded then stuffed the handful of clothing she held into the suitcase and closed it. "I'm ready."

The back door slammed shut and a man's voice reverberated through the house shouting Sarah's name. Jessica sucked in a breath. Were they already too late?

But relief flooded Sarah's face. "Andrew!" She ran to the bedroom door and called out to him. "Andrew, we're here."

He rushed into the room, grabbed Sarah and hugged her tightly. Jessica could see the relief on his face and the affection for the woman now in his arms. But she was shocked to realize she also knew him—Assistant District Attorney Andrew Jennings.

"I'm sorry I wasn't here sooner," he told Sarah. "I was drowning in legal briefs and my phone battery died. I didn't see your messages until this morning. Are you okay?" He touched her face, then her arms, as if checking for himself to make certain she wasn't seriously injured.

"I'm fine. Jessica, this is my brother. Andrew, this is Jessica Taylor. She runs a shelter for women like me."

He turned his eyes from his sister long enough to acknowledge her presence. "We've met."

Yes, they knew one another. They'd worked together in the past and she'd tried with little success to encourage Andrew and the District Attorney's Office to help other victims of domestic violence through stronger charges and higher sentences for batterers.

Andrew Jennings possessed a wide, disarming smile and a charm that put people at ease when he chose to use it. Juries responded to him. The press revered him. And most women swooned at the sight of his sea-green eyes fixed upon her.

But Jessica was not most women.

This man understood high-priced suits and expensive cars. He'd worked his way up the ladder of success in the D.A.'s office by winning cases…and domestic violence cases were hardly ever winnable. He had no clue about what the women in her care endured and no desire to learn. All he cared about was getting his handsome face in the newspaper.

Or so she'd thought until she'd watched him pull Sarah into his strong embrace.

"I won't let him hurt you again. I promise I won't." He looked at Jessica as if to drive home his determination.

He needn't have bothered. The angry flush on his cheeks and the fire in his eyes only confirmed what she already knew. This case was too personal for him to be objective. An altercation between him and Robert would make an already dangerous situation much worse.

After all the cases they'd worked together, why hadn't he come to her when he realized his sister needed help? Did he disdain her so much that he wouldn't even acknowledge she was good at what she did?

"We have to leave. I called the courthouse after I got your messages. Robert posted bail. He's on his way here now. Let's go. My car is parked out front."

Andrew grabbed Sarah's suitcase from the bed then led her toward the living room. Jessica followed behind them, noticing the protective way Andrew's arm never left Sarah's shoulder. This was a side of his nature she'd never seen before.

As he opened the front door, a large white pickup roared into the driveway and a man leaped from the cab. Andrew slammed the door and turned to her. "It's Robert. Now what?"

"While I'm talking to him, you get Sarah to the car. Don't stop moving, even for me." She directed her next command back to Sarah. "Don't speak to him. Don't even look at him. Let your brother lead you out."

The young woman quivered with fear. "What if he comes after me?"

"He'll have to get through me first. And believe me, I won't make it easy for him."

Andrew stepped forward. "Maybe I should be the one to confront him."

"I imagine that would only make things worse." She didn't have time to deal with his macho chivalry. They had to move and fast. "I've dealt with men like Robert before. I can take care of myself." She didn't wait for him to agree. She lengthened her stride as she headed for the front door, silently lifting a prayer that God would guide them to safety.

A shadow on the other side of the window stopped her. Heavy footsteps pounded the concrete. Jessica did a quick assessment. The layout of the room made getting to the back door quickly impossible. She had no choice but to confront him in order to buy time for Andrew and Sarah to escape.

The man who opened the door and blocked their path was thirtyish and built like an NFL linebacker. "Who are you?" he demanded when he saw Jessica. He zeroed in on the suitcase in Andrew's hand then stepped inside and slammed the door. "I knew something was up when I saw Andrew's car out front."

To Jessica's dismay, Sarah ignored her wishes and responded to her husband. "I didn't think you would be here."

He glowered at her. "No, you thought I'd still be in jail, didn't you? Well, they let me go. They said your made-up story about me hitting you was bogus so they had to release me."

Jessica knew his statement was untrue—just more emotional torment—but she saw Sarah shrink at its impact.

"That's a lie." Andrew said, stepping in front of Sarah

in a protective manner. "The judge issued a restraining order against you and you're already in violation of that order by being here. This can send you back to jail."

Robert's nostrils flared in anger and the muscles in his neck flinched. Jessica stepped forward before this could escalate into an altercation between the two men. She hoped the icy stare she flashed Andrew penetrated his thick skull. What part of "don't stop moving" did he not understand? The path to the back door was still clear. "Mr. Young, my name is Jessica. I'm a domestic violence crisis counselor. Sarah has asked for my help."

He had an angry stare that she was certain struck fear in anyone who crossed him. Now, it was specifically reserved for his wife. But that expression quickly faded and in its place a bewildered one emerged. A note of desperation crept into his voice. "What? Why?"

Even though the situation called for a conciliator, the advocate in her fired up. The befuddled look on his face made her ill. These men always liked to play the victim. But she kept her tone deliberate and measured. "You know why."

From the corner of her eye, she spotted Andrew and Sarah finally moving toward the kitchen to escape through the back door.

He shook his head. "Did Andrew bring you here? He's never liked me. He has been trying to turn Sarah against me since the day we met. He tells lies and you believe them."

"No, the bruises on Sarah are all I need to convince me."

"She's clumsy."

Jessica stared him down. "Sure she is."

Robert turned his attention to Sarah and Andrew, who were nearly to the back door. "Sarah!"

"I'm sorry," she cried, stopping and turning back to him. "Please don't be mad."

Andrew reached for her arm and yanked her toward the door. "Sarah, let's go."

Robert turned to intercept them through the front but Jessica matched his steps, firmly blocking his way. Thanks to her added height, she met him nearly eye to eye.

His voice became low and threatening. "Get out of my way."

She refused to be moved. "I won't let you hurt her again."

His jaw clenched and his body stiffened, sure signs that he was getting angry. She knew she should say something to calm him, but those words wouldn't come. This was all too personal now.

"I said, 'Move!'" His big hands jammed her shoulders, pushing her to the floor. Pain seared through her head as it met the edge of the coffee table. A wave of dizziness and nausea swept through her, but she scrambled to get back on her feet. Her eyes refused to focus so Robert was a blur as he took off out the front door and across the lawn chasing after Sarah and Andrew.

Jessica grabbed hold of the table and pulled herself up. She couldn't allow him to reach Sarah. She wouldn't let him hurt her again.

She stumbled a bit as she ran after them but saw Robert reach the car moments after Andrew and Sarah hopped inside. She heard the distinct sound of the door locks and a wave of relief pulsed through her.

Robert pulled on the handle then pounded on the glass. "Get out of the car, Sarah. Open this door and get out now!" His breath caused a fog on the glass. "Get out now or I swear I will kill you. And I'll kill your brother, too!"

She saw Sarah cover her ears to block out his tirade.

As she approached the car, Robert focused his rage on Jessica. "This is your fault. You turned her against me." His hand came out of nowhere and slammed into her face.

Pain ripped through her cheek like a hot searing knife. She stumbled backward and fell to the grass, the hard lawn digging into her hands and knees. She heard heavy breathing as he leaned over her and when Jessica looked up, his muscles were tight and his eyes on fire. His hands were gripped into white-knuckled fists ready to do their damage.

The squeal of the car tires was music to her ears. Jessica blew out a sigh of relief. No matter what happened to her, he would not get to Sarah.

Not tonight.

Not ever again.

"Don't move," Andrew ordered as he hopped from the car. He'd gotten Sarah out of the war zone, but he couldn't let Jessica fight the battle alone. He grabbed his aluminum baseball bat from the athletic bag on the backseat. If Robert wanted a fight, he would get one.

He ran back toward them. Jessica was on the ground kicking and fighting against Robert, who already had her one arm pinned with his knee. He was struggling to contain the other arm. She was a fighter but Andrew knew she wouldn't last long against a big guy like Robert.

"Get away from her!" he yelled, swinging the bat with all his force. Robert fell, clutching his side and groaning in pain.

Andrew stood over him, ready to repay his brother-in-law for the damage he'd done to Sarah. He had Robert in just the position he'd longed for. All the anger and frustration he'd struggled with for months swept through him until he was dizzy with rage and all he could see was the target on Robert's head.

He'd teach him to beat up on his sister.

"Don't do it, Andrew."

The calmness in Jessica's voice reached him through the pent-up indignation. He turned his gaze to her. Her blond hair was matted and red at her temple and her clothes were grass-stained. Blood trickled from her lip and her hose were torn. Yet her countenance was calm, controlled. "Sarah needs you."

He glanced back at the car. Even from this distance, he could see the look of horror on Sarah's face as she climbed into the backseat and watched them through the glass. Yet even after all the stuff Robert had put her through, he was certain her worry was more for the man on the ground than for him.

"Let's go," Jessica said, touching his arm, putting all her focus on pulling him out of this situation. Her touch had a soothing effect and the frenzied fury drained from him.

She'd been right about his confronting Robert. It had definitely made things worse.

Andrew pulled her to her feet then walked beside her, glad for the commanding stride she possessed even after such a beat-down.

"Where's your car?" he asked her.

"Down the road. I'll come back for it later."

He opened the passenger door to his car then closed it once she was safely inside, noticing that Robert was still trying to reclaim his sure footing. Andrew rushed around the car and slid into the driver's seat, dropping the bat at his feet as he started the engine. One glance in the rearview mirror showed Robert crawling to his feet and heading their way.

"This isn't over," he yelled, stumbling toward them. He reached the back of the car and pounded on the trunk. "You think you're through with me? You're worthless, Sarah. Worthless and stupid. You're nothing without me. I'll kill all of you!"

Andrew jammed the car into gear and sped away before the maniac had a chance to make good on his threat. He didn't let up on the accelerator as he sped away from Sarah's neighborhood. He'd always had a heavy foot, but today his speed was purposeful. He had to get his sister as far away from that man as fast as possible.

As he hit the interstate, his adrenaline rush began to cool and his heart rate slowed back to normal. He pushed air through his lungs as he checked his mirrors. There was no sign of Robert following them.

He glanced back at Sarah through the rearview mirror and his heart kicked. She looked so pitiful. It had been only three days since he'd last seen her but she had fresh injuries—a black bruise forming around her left eye and a gash on her swollen lip. And he was sure more bruises were hidden by the baggy clothes she wore. He bit back his anger. "Are you okay?"

She looked ready to fall apart at any moment, but she hugged herself tightly and nodded. "I'm all right."

He couldn't forget the terror that had ripped through him when he'd finally gotten her messages. He'd been locked down working on a case and hadn't charged his phone all night. When he'd finally checked it, he'd found six voice mails from Sarah, each one more hysterical than the previous. She'd been alone with Robert, terrified, with no one to help her.

Help me, Andrew.
I need you.
I'm scared.

Her last call had been from the hospital early this morning to let him know she was okay and that Robert had been arrested, but by the time he'd arrived at the hospital, Sarah had already left, choosing to return home. He'd promised to be there for her, but when it mattered, he'd dropped the ball.

But how had she ended up with Jessica Taylor?

He'd long suspected Jessica had friends on the police force who alerted her when they spotted a woman in trouble. He turned to look at her. She was known to be quick to respond, to offer help. He couldn't deny her passion for her cause. Nothing deterred her from helping those in her care. She was always ready and willing to stick her neck out to help another woman in need. Usually that sort of behavior would strike him as irrational and impulsive, but with his sister's safety on the line, he was glad for Jessica's gutsy determination and passionate devotion to her cause.

She gingerly touched a place on the side of her head. Her hand came back with blood.

Alarm flooded him. "You need to go to the hospital."

"No, I'm fine."

"You're not fine. You're bleeding." He pulled to the side of the road. "Sarah, hand me my gym bag." He dug through it and found a clean towel then pressed it against Jessica's wound, his hand cradling her face. Her skin was soft, softer than he would have ever imagined, softer than he'd expected it to be, given her tough exterior. His fingers brushed her lips accidentally and she trembled but refused to look at him. In fact, she did all she could to avoid looking at him despite how close their faces were.

His gaze perused her heart-shaped face and the slender, regal line of her neck. Strands of long blond hair framed lovely brown eyes and full, pink lips that had never cracked a smile, at least not while he was around.

Everything about her was alluring.

She finally locked eyes with him. "I said I'm fine." She pushed his hand away.

Everything but her holier-than-thou attitude.

He sat back in his seat but held the towel out to her. "Use this to stop the bleeding until we get to the hospital."

"I said no hospital. We need to get your sister to the shelter."

"You need stitches."

"Sarah is my priority. Head downtown," Jessica instructed him.

"Fine." He didn't bother arguing with her. They'd butted heads enough times for him to know that once Jessica Taylor made up her mind there was little chance of changing it, especially when it concerned the safety of someone she'd vowed to protect.

She directed him toward an area off State Street. Tucked between a printing company and a storage facility was a brick office building with the painted title "Dean's Den" on the front. He parked and Jessica jumped out of the car, obviously intent on proving she wasn't hurt. She wobbled a bit but waved off any offer of help. He opened the back door and helped Sarah out. He put his arm around her, noting as he did her small frame. She'd always been petite, but today he could feel her bones. When was the last time she'd eaten?

At the front door, Jessica rang the bell. "Because this is an emergency shelter, we have a lot of different safety measures. This is one of them. No one comes in or out without signing the log."

The door opened and a dark-eyed girl who looked to be no more than twenty let them inside.

"This is my assistant, Mia. If I'm not available she can handle anything you need," Jessica said. "Mia, this is Sarah and her brother. Sarah is going to be staying with us." Jessica continued to spout information as they walked down the hall. "We also have a state-of-the-art alarm system, security monitors and safety glass for the windows."

"Sounds like prison," Sarah muttered beside him.

Jessica, obviously hearing that comment, led them to a window overlooking the common area where several women were gathered around the coffee table while a small child played with blocks on the floor nearby. Jessica's face softened as she addressed Sarah's concerns. "We have a large kitchen, a play area for kids, daily Bible study plus a weekly support group. We're currently housing five other women and four children. You're not a prisoner here, but it is safer for you to remain inside as much as possible."

Sarah nodded her understanding then turned back to staring at the child. Having always wanted children, she had a soft spot for them.

"Would you like to see the rest of the facility?" Jessica asked.

Before Sarah could say yes, Andrew stepped in. "We don't need the tour. I'm taking her home with me."

Jessica's eyes pierced him as she looked his way. "That's a bad idea. We have the resources to protect her. Isn't that what you want?"

He wasn't in the mood to argue. He'd made up his mind. Sarah was not staying. But before he could voice his objection, Sarah spoke.

"She's right. Robert doesn't know about this place. He won't know to look for me here."

"Sarah, I can protect you."

"Staying here sounds a lot safer than being locked up in your apartment. Besides, what about your job? What will I do when you have to go to work? I don't want to be there alone. At least here I have other people to talk to."

He took her hands and squeezed them reassuringly. "We'll work all that out. I want you to come home with me."

She looked to Jessica then slipped her hands from his. "I think this is the best choice for me right now. What if Robert returns and you're not there…like you weren't last night."

All the air left his lungs at her statement. He'd promised to keep her safe and he'd already failed her.

Jessica motioned toward Mia. "Will you show Sarah to a room?"

Sarah turned to go with the girl then ran back to Andrew and hugged him tightly. "Thank you, big brother, for everything. I love you."

The urge to pray for her safety flooded him, a leftover remnant of his old life. He shoved that urge back far down in the depths of his soul. Who would he be praying to, anyway? An absent God that didn't hear his prayers? Or a God that heard but allowed bad things to happen anyway? Prayer had done nothing to save the woman he'd loved, and he wasn't going to depend on it for his sister's safety, either.

He turned to face Jessica. Was he really ready to depend on her to make sure Sarah was out of harm's way?

Jessica, at least, unlike God, had never let him down.

Jessica saw his pained expression as Sarah disappeared around the corner. That look of protectiveness caught her breath as she realized this entire situation was too familiar for comfort.

Overprotective brother.

Vulnerable sister.

And a dangerous, obsessed abuser.

She'd been here before, and it had not turned out well.

"So what do we do now?" Andrew asked turning back to her.

"Now we wait." Jessica motioned him into her office. Once there, she kicked off her heels and enjoyed the coolness of the concrete floor on her tired feet. She slid into her desk chair and watched as Andrew swept her office with a critical eye. It wasn't much. Everything from the couch to the bookshelves had been donated, but Jessica had tried to give the room a homey feel with a few throw rugs and photographs. She'd tried to do the same throughout the shelter. Donated didn't have to mean trashy.

"What do you mean we wait? Wait for what?"

"For Robert to make his move."

"What kind of move?"

"Generally one of three things happen—he'll decide it isn't worth it and move on to someone else—"

"I like that."

"Or he'll see the error of his ways and agree to go to counseling and anger management classes."

She smiled at the way his expression changed from optimistic encouragement to disgust and loathing.

"I don't care for that one, either." She finished her list. "Or he'll continue escalating, in which case we'll have to make different arrangements for Sarah."

"You forgot the one where he goes to jail and stays there."

"I wish it were that simple." She folded her arms and looked at him. He wasn't some ordinary person off the street. He was a prosecutor. He knew better than anyone how the system worked. "You of all people know we're not going to get more than a misdemeanor charge for this assault."

He pulled up a chair and sat down, leaning his elbows into his knees and letting out a long, weary sigh. "I know. But I also know he won't stop. He's—what did you call it—escalating."

"I agree." She'd caught the evil intent in his eye. They hadn't seen the last of him yet. "Tomorrow morning we'll take Sarah down to the precinct so she can give her statement and swear out a complaint against him. She refused to do it at the hospital. It's not much but it might keep him confined a little while longer. I will also notify the police that he violated his restraining order."

"Do I need to be there?"

"No."

"Good. I've got court in the morning."

"Really?" She marveled at how clueless he was. "Didn't you tell Sarah you could protect her if she went home with you? How were going to do that from the courthouse?" She could see his mind working, searching for an answer. Finally, he looked at her, his face set and determined. "I would do anything to get her away from that man." He locked eyes with her. "Anything."

A shiver raced up her spine at his determination to protect Sarah. *Anything* was a dangerous mantra to live by.

"Why didn't you call me? I could have intervened before now."

He pulled his hand through his hair. "I thought I could handle it. I tried to talk to her. I tried to convince her to leave him, but she wouldn't."

She got up and walked around the desk, towered over him as he sat. "What you did, Counselor, was to put me and your sister in jeopardy because you're dealing with a psychology you don't understand."

"I put you in jeopardy?" He rose from his seat. "You placed yourself in a dangerous situation that you didn't need to be in. But that's nothing new for you, is it? Everyone in town knows you thrive on putting yourself at risk."

"You're the one who put me at risk when you didn't get Sarah to the car like I said. You should have been out of the house and in the car before that situation had a chance to escalate."

"What kind of man would I be if I left you to fight that maniac alone?"

Indignation swept through her. How dare he turn this around on her? "Don't give me that macho bravado spin. You wanted him to see you leave with Sarah. You wanted him to know that you were going to stop him."

"I did what I had to do to protect my sister."

Without her heels, she had to look up at him, but that didn't stop her from locking eyes with him and issuing a stern warning. "Your form of protection is going to get someone killed."

She didn't realize she was yelling until a voice from the doorway interrupted their conversation. "Children, children, behave." They both turned at the reproach. Her friend Margo was standing in the doorway. She'd been the first friend Jessica made when she came to Jackson from Atlanta. She'd been instrumental in helping start and fund the shelter. Slim and athletic, she didn't need the badge or gun at her hip to exude authority. It flowed from her personality.

Margo stepped between them. "I'm calling a time-out for you two kids. What's going on?"

"Nothing." They both spoke in unison then turned away. She glanced at Jessica and smirked as if knowing how childish Jessica felt at that moment. Margo always treated her like a mother hen and now she'd caught her playing tug-of-war with the school yard bully.

"Margo, this is Andrew Jennings. Andrew, this is my friend Detective Margo Stephens."

He held out his hand but all Margo returned was a cold stare. "I know who you are. You let Tim Meadows slide with a three-month probation on misdemeanor assault."

He pulled his hand back. "We almost didn't get that. As I recall, Mrs. Meadows refused to testify about how she received her injuries. All we had to prosecute was the bystander he punched."

She turned back to Jessica. "What's he doing here?"

"I'm helping his sister." She saw the surprised look Margo gave her. "Sarah needs help, regardless of who her brother is."

Margo's eyes widened and she rushed to Jessica's side. "You're bleeding."

Jessica touched the spot on her head. The pain had already faded from a jackhammer into an ice pick jabbing into one spot on her temple. "It's nothing. I'm fine."

"I'm taking you to the hospital right now."

She pulled away from Margo's grasp, hating being treated like a child for the second time today. "No, I'm going home. I can't wait for a long soak in a hot bath. After that, I'll be fine."

"Well, where is your car? It wasn't in the parking lot."

She'd forgotten. They'd left in Andrew's car. "I had to leave it."

Margo sighed. "Give me the address. I'll go get it and bring it to you after my shift ends."

She scribbled down the address and handed it to Margo along with a spare set of keys.

"I'll take you home," Andrew offered.

Margo turned to him. "She is not going anywhere with you, Counselor."

Usually, Jessica didn't allow anyone to know where she lived, but Andrew wasn't just anyone. She knew him and despite their differences on past cases, he wasn't the type to hand out her private address.

Plus his offer would save her from the loving rebuke Margo was sure to give her on the car ride to her house.

You have to be more careful, Jessica.

You have to think about your safety, Jessica.

Her friend meant well, but Jessica was too tired and too sore to argue tonight. "Thank you for the offer, Andrew. I accept."

Margo shot her a curious look but didn't belabor the point. "I'll see you later, then."

Jessica let Mia know they were leaving then walked with Andrew to his car.

But as he opened the passenger door for her and she slid inside, she realized how uncharacteristically quick she'd agreed to let him drive her. She'd trusted him so easily and not only because she knew him in a professional sense. She'd seen beneath the shell of the man he projected to the media and the courtroom and she'd caught a glimpse into his soul. Since the moment he'd pulled Sarah into his arms, ever since she'd seen the protectiveness in him, her opinion of him had been altered. He was no longer just the spoiled rich golden boy of the D.A.'s office. He was more than that now. He now possessed a quality that made him even more attractive than good looks or charm or expensive suits could ever do.

Or had he always had that quality and she'd just never noticed?

She recalled that moment in the car when he'd touched her face, his fingers gentle and nimble on her wound.

He'd leaned so close she could hear the pounding of his heart and feel the warmth of his breath on her skin. Her heart fluttered at the memory just as it had at the moment.

She blew out a breath and turned her head away as Andrew started the car and drove.

Maybe getting into the car with him again wasn't such a good idea. She had to remain strong and in control. She wouldn't allow herself to become one of the many women falling over themselves to get Andrew Jennings to notice her.

TWO

Jessica directed him toward a subdivision outside of town. The neighborhood seemed quaint and quiet with rows of older houses. Jessica pointed to a white single-storied house with a large front porch as hers.

He parked in the driveway, then shut off the engine.

"Thank you for the ride," she said, then opened the door and hopped out without waiting for him.

"I'll walk you to the door," Andrew said, getting out and following her.

She stopped him at the porch steps. "That's not necessary."

"I should be going, anyway. Thank you for your help with Sarah today. I've been trying for months to get her to leave Robert. You're right. I should have come to you sooner."

She stopped him as he turned to walk away. "Why didn't you?"

For months he'd worried about Sarah, pleaded with her to get help. He'd even picked up the phone to call Jessica several times. He shrugged and admitted the truth. "You and I have been at odds so many times I suppose I was afraid you might turn me away, and I didn't know what I would do if you did that."

"Andrew, we've had our disagreements over cases, but why would you think I would turn you down? We're not enemies. We're both on the same side—helping people." She reached for his hand and squeezed it and a singe of electricity rushed through him, kick-starting his pulse into high gear. Her touch had had a calming effect on him earlier but was now having the opposite effect.

"Really? Tell that to your friend Margo."

"Margo is just very passionate. She knew Alicia Meadows. She'd counseled her several times. Then, she was one of the detectives who responded to the scene the day Tim Meadows shot her then himself."

"I wish I could have done more to protect her. If there had been anything else—"

"You did what you could. Sometimes the law just isn't enough."

He didn't like the sound of that. Was she implying she would go outside the law to protect those in her care?

Or that she had?

Jessica spun at the crunch of leaves on the other side of the porch. He saw her—felt it really—tense. Her eyes widened and she gripped the railing. He would almost say it was fear that crossed her face.

But before he could check to see who was approaching, he heard the distinct yapping of a dog.

Jessica seemed to relax at that sound. "It's just my next door neighbor."

A moment later, a robust, elderly, grandmotherly type woman appeared in the light, a tiny Yorkshire on a leash yapping and dancing at her feet. "Hush, Marlon," she scolded the dog.

Jessica leaned over the railing. "Hello, Mrs. Brady. How are you tonight?"

She smiled a genuine smile that stretched across her face. "I'm doing very well, Jessica. I was in a baking mood today so I made this for the girls at the shelter. I thought they could use a little treat." She handed Jessica the cake plate she was carrying. "It's Pineapple Upside Down cake."

"I'm sure they'll love it, Mrs. Brady. Thank you."

The older woman glanced up at him. The look of curiosity on her face told him that finding Jessica with a man at her house wasn't a common occurrence.

Jessica was quick to introduce him. "This is A.D.A. Andrew Jennings. We are working on a case together."

"It's nice to meet you, Mrs. Brady."

"Yes, nice to meet you, too." She turned back to Jessica. "My ladies' group is also knitting some mittens for the children. I know it's warm today but we've already had two cold snaps and it's only October."

"That's very kind of you. I know they'll appreciate it."

Mrs. Brady aimed her next comments toward him. "Since Mr. Brady passed away I haven't had much to occupy my days except doing for others. I wasn't blessed with children of my own so I've got no grandbabies to spoil. My sister has been hounding me for years to move in with her, but all her family is up north and it's too cold there. No, Marlon and I are very happy here, aren't we, Marlon?"

The little dog yapped his response.

"Would you like to come inside for a moment?"

"No, thank you. I'm right in the middle of pounding out pie crusts. I was watching out my window to make sure I saw when you came home. I wanted to catch you to give you that cake." She picked up her dog. "I really should get back. Take care."

Jessica watched until she and Marlon made it to her house. She placed the dish on the railing. "Her kitchen overlooks my yard so she can see people coming or going."

"It's nice to have people watching out for you."

"In my line of work it's a necessity. Who knows when some angry, vengeful husband or boyfriend might decide to follow me home? I have all the necessary precautions— alarm system, dead bolts, timed lights, even an automatic garage-door opener—but it's still nice to know I've got another pair of eyes looking out for me."

"I guess you make a lot of enemies in your job. You certainly made one in Robert today."

"I know. It's a risk of my job."

A risk she was only too willing to take. *Just like Tory.* "I should go. I have to be in court tomorrow morning. I'm in the middle of a case."

"Yes, the Trevino trial. How is that going?"

"Good. Jury selection is over. We start opening remarks tomorrow."

"I'll be at the courthouse tomorrow. Maybe I'll see you."

He nodded then turned and walked away. He avoided looking back at the house as he headed to his car but heard the sound of the door close.

His brain swam with conflicting thoughts. He'd worked with Jessica many times before and her presence had never elicited this kind of reaction in him. In fact, she usually had the effect of annoying and frustrating him in their dealings. But today something had been different between them, something that had left him both electrified and apprehensive at the same time.

He'd spent the two years since Tory's death throwing

himself into work and avoiding personal contact. Today, he'd crossed that boundary without even seeing the line.

It was time to focus on his case again. But at least he knew Sarah was in good hands.

Jessica hit the light switch and scanned the room carefully before coming inside and locking the door behind her. Nothing seemed out of place. The butterfly on her prayer quilt was upright on her chair. The books on the window ledge were in order by title. No one would get through the window without her knowing. Her laptop was closed, the pen intentionally placed atop it still in its position.

Yet she had the eerie feeling someone was watching her and she thought she smelled men's cologne.

Get a grip, Jessica.

It was probably only the aftereffects of her confrontation with Robert Young, but her emotions were on edge.

She checked the rest of the house but found no evidence that anyone had been there. Convinced she was imagining the strange scent, she set the pineapple upside down cake on the coffee table, certain Mrs. Brady had brought over that cake only as a means to check on her. It wasn't every day— In fact, she'd never before brought a man to her home.

She should have invited him in for coffee. It was innocent and she trusted Andrew. And after the day's events with Robert Young, the house seemed so dark and empty. She was tired of doing her usual routine of checking behind every door and inside every closet just to assure herself that no one was there. For once, she wanted to return home without being afraid.

Dean's Den was her baby, her ministry, but even though she routinely stayed there for days on end, she enjoyed having a home of her own, a sanctuary where she could hide out and recharge after confronting so much violence and suffering.

But lately, she'd been praying about whether or not to keep it.

Was it right for her to have such a place when those she counseled had none? She sighed, thinking of the greater benefit her rent money could go to——new bed sheets, more games for the kids, another counseling room.

And even though she'd felt God leading her in that direction, He hadn't yet provided her the clear sign she needed to make the change.

She was usually keyed up after a difficult confrontation, but something about this encounter felt different to her. She'd taken out her frustration on Andrew back at the shelter but truthfully it was herself she was mad at. She'd lost her professionalism. She'd looked into Robert's eyes and seen a familiar face——a face that still haunted her even after all this time.

Mitch.

She rubbed her hand over the goose egg on her temple. Why was all this coming up now? It had more to do with Andrew than it did with Robert. He reminded her so much of Dean in the way he'd held on to Sarah. He'd risked his life and his career to help her.

Just as Dean had once done for her.

She picked up the photograph of her brother from the bookcase. She and Andrew didn't always have to see eye to eye for her to help him. Whatever she had to do she vowed she would do it. She would not allow Andrew to give up his life to protect Sarah.

Her stomach clutched as a wave of loneliness enveloped her. She was twenty-six years old. Her heart insisted that was too young to give up on love, but her mind knew better. She'd already been down that road once before only to have it end in tragedy. She had no illusions about love and relationships.

Yet when she'd stared into Andrew's fierce green eyes...

She pushed those thoughts away. Of course he was handsome. Every woman in the television viewing area knew he was handsome.

But she would never again be fooled by a handsome face and boyish charm.

Leslie Wells, the receptionist at the district attorney's office, met Andrew as he walked through the door. "He wants to see you."

Andrew glanced at his watch. He'd been gone for several hours after getting Sarah's messages. He didn't even bother going to his office first to drop off his coat and briefcase. He knocked on Bill's door then stepped inside. "You wanted to see me?"

Bill Foster leaned back in his chair, folded his arms and studied Andrew. "You didn't answer my calls."

"I know. I apologize. I had an emergency.

"You know who does return my calls? Jason Clark. He said you didn't come back after the lunch recess then went missing most of the afternoon."

Andrew grimaced. Jason Clark was a first-year attorney fresh out of law school with a lot of ambition and an oversize ego. "I had an emergency with my sister." He hated using that excuse again but he had no choice. He'd kept Bill in the loop about what was happening with Sarah and, so far, his boss had been reasonable about giving him the necessary time. But with the election season about to go into full swing and Bill eyeing the state's attorney general position, Andrew knew he had to watch his step. "I can assure you everything is fine now. Sarah is safe and my focus is now solely on this trial."

"This is a big case for our office, Andrew. A conviction could do a lot to benefit your career."

Brian Trevino was a career criminal with multiple counts of home invasion on his rap sheet. He'd already served two stretches for burglary at Parchman Prison and now he was on trial for two counts of homicide related to a home invasion where he'd killed a fifty-two-year-old couple when they awoke and discovered him inside their home. A conviction would do wonders for Bill's campaign.

"We're ready."

"Good. I'll be stopping by the courthouse tomorrow. I think I'll bring CJ along with me and let her see how a good trial lawyer does his job."

Andrew understood his meaning. CJ Bennett was another up-and-coming attorney in the office. She'd been biting at Andrew's tail to grab the biggest and most profiled cases she could get. She was hungry to make a name for herself. Bill's not-so-veiled threat was clear— do a good job on the trial or he might find his attentions turning toward CJ instead of him.

"I won't let you down, Bill."

"I hope not, for your sake."

Andrew accepted the admonishment and left. He dropped his coat in his office as he gathered his files. His team was scheduled to meet in the conference room for a last-minute strategy session. And the number one item on Andrew's agenda for the meeting was to ream Jason Clark about squealing to the boss.

* * *

Jessica's cell phone buzzed, alerting her to a message. She checked it and saw it was from Margo. Perhaps she hadn't gotten out of that rebuke, after all.

Her friend was at the door a moment later. "I cannot believe you did that," Margo said, storming into the house. The disapproving look on her face was not surprising. It was no secret what her friend was referring to—going to Sarah's house alone.

"It was an emergency situation. The husband was escalating. The wife needed to get out. I saw an opening and I took it."

"You should have called me before you went over there. Did Mr. 'Oh, I'm so wonderful' convince you to go?"

"No, actually, I have a friend in the Pearl Police Department who called me. He said Robert Young was a maniac, and he was right. Sarah was in real danger staying there. Andrew has reason to be concerned about her."

"That man doesn't even know the meaning of the phrase 'real danger.'"

Margo stopped and glanced around. "Is he here?"

"Of course not. Why?"

"I smell men's cologne."

Jessica shuddered. So she hadn't been imagining it. "I noticed it too when I came in."

Margo placed her hand on the weapon at her hip as she scanned the room. She walked cautiously toward the kitchen and glanced around before moving to the desk. She pushed through the stack of mail until she reached a postcard. As she sniffed it, her body relaxed and she released the hold on her gun.

"For a moment, I thought you'd invited Mr. Hottie A.D.A. over for coffee."

Jessica saw the card was an advertisement for men's cologne complete with a sample scent. She felt heat rise in her face both at her silly concerns and the insinuation Margo made. "Don't be ridiculous."

"Why is that ridiculous? I saw the way you two were going at it in your office."

"We were arguing. The man is intolerable. All he cares about is getting his handsome face in the newspaper." She felt heat rise in her face as she realized that despite their previous interactions and the opinions she'd had about him until now, she could no longer say that.

Margo grinned. "So you think he's handsome?"

Jessica snatched the card from her. "I think he thinks he's handsome." She sniffed the card, remembering the musky scent of Andrew's aftershave. "What I know is he has no idea what the women we counsel endure and no desire to learn. He didn't want Sarah to stay. He still thinks he can handle this all himself."

"Well he was right about one thing—you placed yourself in a dangerous situation…again. I wish you'd let me teach you to shoot."

Margo was always pushing her to buy a gun, but each time Jessica considered it, she flashed back to that terrible night five years earlier. Dean had spent hours with her at the gun range, but all the training in the world hadn't done her any good at the moment it really mattered. "Margo, I appreciate the self-defense lessons, but I'm just not comfortable around guns."

"You deal with dangerous men. You need to do a better job of protecting yourself."

"I take all the precautions I can."

"You should stay at the shelter."

Jessica gave a weary sigh. "If it were up to you, I'd live at the shelter."

"You'd be safer."

Safety, she'd learned, too often became a prison. That was something Margo didn't yet understand. She was still too tied up in her own pain and fear.

Margo gave her a piercing look, obviously realizing she wasn't going to get anywhere. She stood to leave. "I should go. I had a rookie follow me here. He's waiting in the car. Promise me you'll be careful."

"I'm always careful." She closed and locked the door behind her friend then reset the alarm.

She sniffed the postcard, relieved this was the origination of the scent. Why hadn't she thrown that away yesterday with the rest of her junk mail? She had no desire to purchase men's cologne.

She had no one to purchase it for.

Jessica had a busy morning ahead of her. She couldn't afford the headache that insisted on hanging on overnight. She swallowed two pain relievers then tossed the bottle into her purse. She had a feeling she would be needing it again to get through the day.

She called the shelter to check on things. Mia updated her on the goings-on including heated words between two of their residents—Joan Ratliff, a pregnant mother with a two-year-old, and Amber Wade, a mother of three who'd fled her alcoholic husband for the third time. "What happened there?"

"Just rising tension. Danielle stepped in and calmed them down."

Jessica was glad for the assistance of Danielle Manchester, a young college-aged girl whose boyfriend had beaten and stalked her. Danielle was always quick to help care for Joan's baby or occupy Amber's kids. Still, four children under eight years old confined to a small area

was bound to grate on everyone's nerves. Tensions were
certain to rise. "Maybe it would be a good idea to take
the kids to the park today. Just don't forget to take your
cell phone in case there's trouble."

"There's one more thing," Mia said.

Jessica heard the hesitation in her voice. "What is it?"

"It's Sarah. She's determined she's not going to press
charges against her husband. She's worried about him
going to jail."

Jessica sighed, disappointed but not really surprised.
It wasn't uncommon for a battered wife to refuse to press
charges.

"Reassure her that she doesn't have to press charges
to stay at the shelter. I'll try to talk to her too when I get
there."

"She wanted me to ask if you would be the one to tell
her brother."

This wasn't the first time she'd been asked to step between families, but it was the first time she'd hesitated.
She knew from their conversation the night before that
Sarah was right—Andrew would not be happy with her
decision. He probably wouldn't be too happy with Jessica, either. But he wasn't the one she'd promised to protect. Sarah was her client and she had to do the best she
could for her.

"I'll talk to him," she promised, already knowing how
she would regret that conversation.

She hung up then tossed her phone into her purse,
slid on her coat and grabbed her laptop and a stack of
papers she had to attend to today. She locked the door
behind her. Her car was in the driveway, and she said a
silent prayer of thanks to Margo for taking care of getting it home to her.

A layer of frost covered the lawn and a bitter wind

tousled her hair. She pulled her jacket tight and stepped off the porch, scanning the yard and street for anything out of the ordinary. She quickened her pace as she headed toward her car.

She stopped before she reached it, noticing the line of footprints in the frosty grass.

She glanced around again but saw nothing and no one unusual in the area. But someone had been in her yard, near her car. The footprints followed the line of the driveway, stopping at the end of the porch.

Someone had been here.

She cautiously approached her car, scanning for broken glass, slashed tires or anything out of the ordinary. It looked fine. She tried the door but found it locked as it should have been. A quick glance into the backseat revealed no one crouched behind the seat. She hated that her mind automatically went in that direction, but the footprints did seem to indicate an intruder in her yard.

"Good morning, Jessica."

She startled at her name and her heart raced. It was only Mr. Percy, her elderly neighbor from two houses down, out for his morning stroll.

"Mr. Percy, how are you today?"

"I can't complain. I'm surprised to see you out and about. You should tell your friend to park your car in the garage next time. A pretty young girl like you doesn't need to be coming and going late at night like you sometimes do without taking precautions."

Trepidation filled her. "You watch me?"

"Well, I don't sleep all that well so I pay attention to any car that comes down this street at night. We can't be too careful these days, can we?"

That explained the feeling she'd had lately of being observed. It had only been the watchful eyes of sweet old Mr. Percy. Why didn't that soothe her nerves? "You haven't noticed anyone in my yard, have you?" She pointed out the footprints. "Have you seen anything odd lately? Anyone around the neighborhood that doesn't belong?"

"No, can't say I have. You know I did see Mrs. Cowart's son out walking the dog this morning. It's possible the little guy got away from him and he chased him into your yard."

Jessica stared at the footprints. They didn't look as if they'd been made by a fourteen-year-old's foot. But how big did a teenage boy's feet get? She didn't know.

"I'll let you get going," he said. "Have a blessed day."

"You, too. Goodbye, Mr. Percy."

She waved to him then walked back to her car. She stared at the footprints and felt silly for overreacting again. They didn't have to mean anything. Perhaps Mr. Percy was right and some neighbor had been chasing a loose pet during an early-morning walk. After all, she'd heard nothing during the night. She shook off her fears. There was nothing sinister about this situation. So someone had been in her yard. It was probably an innocent matter, certainly nothing to freak out about.

She hopped into her car and started it quickly before the paranoia overtook her. She hated the way she kept reverting back to it. She couldn't continue to allow Mitch to have such control over her. Would she never overcome her past? Would she never be free from fear?

Knowing Andrew would be in court most of the day, Jessica spent the morning trying to convince Sarah to press charges against her husband, but nothing she said would change the young woman's mind. Sarah was scared and hurt, but she was still clinging to her loyalty to her husband. Unfortunately, Jessica had seen this type of misplaced loyalty many times before.

Finally, Jessica could stall no more. It was time to face Andrew and break the news to him about Sarah's decision. She drove to the courthouse and parked. After locating the courtroom where the Trevino trial was taking place, she slipped inside and took a seat near the back, hoping she could catch a moment to speak to Andrew during a break.

This wasn't the first time she'd seen him in prosecutor mode, but it was the first time she'd had no ties to the case so she had no reason to analyze his tactics. Instead, she watched the length of his stride, the swagger in his step and the way he charmed the jury with his boyish grin as he made opening remarks. The case he portrayed sounded solid. She glanced at the jury members. They were responding to him, watching him as he moved, leaning forward to hang on his every word. They trusted him.

She smiled. She understood their reaction. It was easy to trust him.

He caught her eye when he turned. A small smile played on his lips. Her face burned with embarrassment, knowing she'd been admiring not his work but his physical presence. And he'd just caught her doing it.

When the judge recessed for the day, Andrew scooped up his briefcase and headed her way. "Hi, Jessica, do you have an interest in this case?"

She felt her face redden as she realized the only interest she had in this case was standing right in front of her. "Not really. I need to talk to you."

His brows scrunched in worry. "Did something happen to Sarah?" He pulled out his phone to check his messages.

"Sarah's fine." Jessica reached her hand out to stop

him, but when her fingers touched his arm, a jolt of electricity caused her to momentarily forget what she wanted to say. She stared up into his questioning eyes as he waited for her to finish. "There is something we need to discuss."

He glanced at his watch then back at a group of people standing across the room. Jessica recognized one of them as the district attorney.

"If now isn't a good time, we can talk later."

"No. Let's talk now." He took her arm and led her through the doors of the courtroom.

"This won't take long."

He led her to a bench outside the courtroom and they took a seat. Jessica noticed the D.A. glancing toward them.

"If you really need to go..." She pointed his way.

He shook his head. "I'll catch up with him later. What's going on?"

"It's Sarah. She is refusing to press charges against Robert. She won't testify against him either if the D.A.'s office decides to pursue the case."

His whole body seemed to clench. "What? Why?"

"She's afraid. It's not an uncommon phenomenon."

"I'll talk to her."

The sternness in his tone bit at her. "You can't bully her into making this decision. She has to take these steps on her own."

"I'm not going to bully her. I'm just going to help her along."

She knew his kind of "helping." "You can't do that."

"Why not? I'm her brother."

"You just can't. All you'll do is push her away."

He grumbled and rubbed his face. Frustration dripped

from every muscle. "I don't even understand my sister anymore."

"Control is a difficult thing to give up."

"It's better than giving up your life, isn't it?"

"Said the man who is always in control." Her thoughts slipped into words before she had a chance to stop them, but she didn't care. The condescension in his voice rubbed her wrong. Who was he to judge anyone? He'd never been in Sarah's situation.

Or hers.

"Wait a minute. How did this turn around to be about me? I haven't done anything but try to help Sarah."

"You judge her for the choices she's made."

"She's made bad choices. That's not my fault."

"No, but a little understanding wouldn't hurt. Isn't she paying a high enough price? She doesn't need her perfect brother looking down his nose at her, as well." Jessica hopped up so fast she knocked over his briefcase.

Even as she stomped away she knew she was being irrational. Just being with him, listening to him, dredged up memories she'd tried to bury for years. It wasn't Andrew's fault, yet he was catching the blame.

He reminded her so much of Dean with his protective nature and the frustration in his voice. Dean hadn't known how to help her, just as Andrew was finding it hard to take care of Sarah. She should be trying to make it easier for them both but instead she was struggling herself. After all these years, after all the families she'd counseled, why was this coming up now? And, more important, how did she stop it from happening so she could focus on her job?

She rushed down the courthouse steps and walked quickly toward her car, aware that Andrew was behind her. She couldn't—wouldn't—let him see the tears pressing to let loose.

She stopped as she neared her car and noticed something on her windshield. Beneath the wiper, she spotted a white envelope. It wouldn't have caught her attention as anything more than a flyer if a bright red rose wasn't sitting on top of it.

Andrew caught up to her. "We need to talk about this. What did I say that upset you?"

She ignored his question and pulled the envelope from the windshield. Her name was typed in the center. She tore open the seal and pulled out a folded piece of paper. The note was typed and unsigned, but the five little words stopped her cold. She quickly scanned the area. No familiar faces jumped out at her, but someone had been at her car. Someone had left this note for her to find. This she couldn't write off as paranoia.

Andrew noticed her demeanor. He reached out and touched her arm. "You're shaking." His voice grew stern. "What's the matter?"

She held out the note and he read it.

You can't stop true love.

Someone was out there taunting her, watching her, stalking her. And no one knew better than Jessica not to take this threat lightly.

THREE

A scowl formed on Andrew's face as he read the note again. "There's no signature. Do you have any idea who this is from?"

She shook her head. "I don't know."

"Who knew you were coming to the courthouse today?"

She struggled to think clearly. Who had she told about her plans? "Mia, of course. Anyone at the shelter." Had she mentioned it to Mr. Percy? "I don't know, but I come to the courthouse several times a week. Anyone who works here would know that."

"You couldn't have been inside for more than an hour after you parked. That's not a lot of time to track down your car and leave this note without being seen."

"Do you think whoever did this was…" She took a steadying breath as she realized where his logic was headed. "He could have followed me from my house." She thought about the footprints in her yard earlier that she had been too quick to dismiss. "I think you're right. I think he followed me here." She told him about the footprints.

"Did you call the police?"

"No. I felt foolish even telling my neighbor. He convinced me it was probably someone from the neighborhood chasing after a pet." She mentally kicked herself. Why had she allowed Mr. Percy to soothe her suspicions so quickly? She should have trusted her instincts when they told her something was wrong. She pulled out her phone. "I'll call Margo."

It took only minutes before a patrol car stopped beside them. Margo's unmarked car squealed to a stop behind the patrol car. She hopped out and was at Jessica's side in an instant. "Jessica, are you alright?"

"I'm okay," Jessica assured her.

"She found this on her car," Andrew said showing her the note and envelope. "We both touched the letter but neither of us touched the rose."

Margo scanned the paper. "Do you have any idea who could have left this?"

She shook her head.

Margo took command. "Well, whoever left it had to touch the windshield wiper. I'll have the car towed to the garage so the forensics team can dust it for prints. An officer will drive you to the shelter."

Jessica stood up. "I'm going home."

"I'll take her," Andrew offered.

Margo glanced her way waiting for her say no, but once again she was truthfully glad for the offer.

"I would appreciate that."

"I'll go get my car." He returned moments later, pulling up in his silver sedan and opening the door for her.

As she slid into the passenger's seat, she admired the feel of the leather and was reminded again of how very different they were. Andrew lived in a world of high-priced cars and expensive suits. She juggled bills and begged for donations in order to keep the shelter running month-to-month. Yet they both saw the worst of the world and fought against it.

In that way, they were kindred spirits.

Maybe even more so now that he was learning first-hand the dangers of her life.

She'd seen a different side of him with his sister. Was it possible Andrew Jennings was more than he seemed?

She was glad when he pulled up to her house. She gathered her papers, trying to gather up her courage as well and hating the way her heart skipped at the thought of approaching the house knowing that someone had been in her yard this morning. This was her home, yet some-one was purposefully trying to make her afraid to enter her own house.

"I'll walk you to the door." He got out, circled the car and opened the door for her.

Her initial instinct was to insist she didn't need it, but truthfully she was thankful for the offer...and for the steadying hand on her arm. She felt better having him with her to face the empty house and having his strong presence beside her.

She only hoped he couldn't feel her shaking or if he could, that he would think it was because she was fright-ened and not because his touch sent shivers through her.

She stopped him at the porch steps. "I'm good from here. Thanks." He was already getting too close for com-fort.

The afternoon light cast a soft glow over his face as he eyed her. "Are you sure? You're shaking. Let me walk you to the door."

"I'm fine. It's just been a very long few days."

"I know what you mean. I couldn't even sleep last night. After our confrontation with Robert, I was so wired. I couldn't settle down. That must be how you feel all the time with the risks you take."

"I try not to take risks."

"You can't deny in your line of work you make enemies. You certainly made one in Robert."

She couldn't deny his assertion but it didn't help alleviate her ever-growing paranoia. Was it possible Robert or any one of the husbands or boyfriends of the women she took in was purposefully taunting her? "My job may have certain risks, but I try to keep my personal and professional lives separate." And Andrew was definitely part of her professional life despite how close she felt to him right now. She moved up onto the porch step away from him to accentuate her point. "Thank you for bringing me home. Good night."

"Good night."

She ducked her head beneath the wind chimes she'd strategically hung low to alert her when someone stepped onto her porch and headed for the door, stopping as something crunched under her feet. Andrew hopped up onto the porch, hitting the chimes and sending them wailing. She jumped, startled by the noise. That haunting sound of metal on metal always struck fear in her. He stopped them with his hand, but it didn't stop the thunderous pounding of her heart.

She leaned against the railing for support as he quickly apologized then knelt down and picked up a piece of whatever was on the floor of her porch.

"It's glass shards," he said glancing up.

She followed his gaze toward the light mounted by the door and knew it was likely the shattered remains of the bulb. The afternoon sun cast a shadow on the porch, making it difficult to see the shards. She quickly unlocked the door and clicked the wall switch for the living room.

Light flowed from inside the house, illuminating the porch enough to see shattered pieces of white tinted glass.

Someone had been on her porch.

Someone had purposefully broken her light.

Andrew stood and peered beneath the porch light mount. Only the stem of the bulb remained screwed into the socket. "It probably just shattered," he said, seeing how her face went blank with shock at the idea that someone had been on her porch.

Their discussion about making enemies must be weighing on her mind. Why had he said that? He tried to put her mind at ease. "It was probably a bad bulb. It's not uncommon."

"No. I know." But the way she clutched her arms together and the furrow of her brow told him she was rattled by the event…and after the day she'd had, who could blame her for being shaken.

"Do you want me to take a look inside, check the house for you?"

"No, really, it's fine. I'm fine." She made a brave showing, but the tremor in her voice belied her comments. "I'll go get the broom." He watched her walk inside, stopping and staring at her desk for several moments as if something was out of place, as if someone had been inside. Finally, she touched a photograph and moved it ever so slightly before disappearing into the kitchen. She returned a moment later with a replacement bulb as well as a broom and dustpan. He screwed in the new bulb then helped her sweep up the broken glass.

"Look, Jessica, I didn't mean to imply earlier that you could be in any danger."

"I know."

"It's just I think you take too many risks."

"I do what I have to do. It's my job."

"But that's the point. It is just a job."

Despite her fearful expression, she shook her head. "Not to me."

He finished sweeping up the glass then moved toward the end of the porch. His head hit the wind chimes, causing them to sound again. Uneasiness flitted through her eyes at the sound. He was beginning to suspect she'd booby-trapped the porch.

It struck him then. She was afraid. She recognized the seriousness of her job. She took precautions because she understood the risks. "I think Margo is right. It's better if you stay at the shelter."

Her face grew firm with determination as she pushed through the fear. "I won't be run out of my home. If I hide then they win."

"They?"

"They. Them. These men who get their thrills terrorizing women. I'm a little rattled, I admit, but I'm okay. We don't know for certain the footprints were from anyone other than a neighbor, and whoever left that note on my car is just trying to frighten me. I'll lock the house up tight and activate the alarm after you leave."

He saw through her bravado, but she'd obviously made up her mind. She was staying. "I'd feel better about leaving if you'd let me check the house."

She glanced inside then nodded and moved from the door.

He doubted anyone was lurking in the closets waiting to attack, but he'd learned from Robert that people often did things that surprised him. He'd never underestimate anything anyone could do again.

He checked every room and found nothing. Whoever was after her hadn't gotten inside yet. Was it true what she said? Were the note and flower only meant to frighten her? She was the expert...but his gut told him differently.

He made his way back to the front of the house. Jessica was still standing on the porch, chewing nervously on her fingernail. All color had drained from her face and she was shivering. He doubted it was from the chill in the night air.

"All clear."

She stepped inside as he stepped out. Still, he didn't relish the idea of leaving her here alone. "Lock this door when I leave."

"I will."

He considered asking her once more to stay at the shelter then decided against it. She'd made her decision clear. "Can I phone you later to make sure you're okay?"

"I would like that."

He waited until she was inside and he heard the click of the door locks and the beep of the alarm before he stepped off the porch, careful to miss the wind chimes. As he walked to his car, he glanced back at the house and saw her peeking at him through the curtains. She was frightened, but she was standing her ground. He admired her tenacity. She reminded him of Tory in a lot of ways. They were both tough and independent with a drive to take risks. They hated to be thought of as weak. But Tory had taken the notion of risk-taking to the extreme and paid the ultimate price for her foolishness.

Foolish risks. That was a trait Tory and Jessica shared.

He shook his head. Why was he comparing the woman he'd loved to Jessica Taylor? Why had his mind even thought about her in that way? He wasn't yet ready for that kind of relationship again. It hadn't been long enough since Tory's death. And besides, even if he were prepared to jump back into the dating pool, it wouldn't be with someone like Jessica who took such risks with her safety.

Yet as he drove off, he couldn't stop remembering the softness of her skin as he'd held her face in his hands.

Andrew stopped by the deli at the grocery store to pick up dinner. He wasn't in the mood to cook and the deli always had a hot meal ready and the food was good.

As he headed for the deli, someone called his name. He glanced around to see Tom Ridley waving and pushing a loaded grocery cart toward him.

Tom was a defense attorney and a friend from church—back in the days when Andrew still attended—when he was part of a couple who attended the Sunday-school couples class run by Tom and his wife, Olivia.

Andrew shook his outstretched hand. "Tom, how are you?"

"Great. Olivia and I were talking about you the other day. We see you more on the news now than we see the newscasters. Good job snagging the Trevino case."

"Thank you."

"We'd love to see you at church again sometime. I'm heading up a men's class now. Unless you've been attending elsewhere?"

"No, not really." He hadn't set foot inside a church since Tory's death, and he had no desire to change that. But he did miss seeing his friends. Tom and Olivia had been there for him during the good times and the bad. "How is Olivia?"

"Great. She'd love to see you. Why don't you come over for supper?"

He perked up, excited about the opportunity to spend time with his old friends. His excitement waned as he remembered that Tom had the life he'd always wanted—

wife, kids, family, a complete future that had been placed on hold by Tory's death. He wasn't sure he was ready yet to sit through a night watching his friends enjoy the life he'd never have. "I'll do that one day soon."

Tom seemed to notice the change. "Well, any night is fine. We need to catch up."

"We do. Tell Olivia I said hello."

Tom walked away, but seeing him reminded Andrew of how his life had changed over the past two years. He'd pulled away from relationships in all areas including friends and family. He'd thrown himself into his work, putting in sixteen-hour days and honing his skills as a prosecutor. As a result, he'd worked his way up the ladder of success in the District Attorney's Office.

Deciding he wasn't hungry after all, he started back to his car, his mind rolling over the changes that had taken place. His life had altered without his consent, with circumstances beyond his control.

"Andrew!"

He turned to see a familiar white pickup screeching to a halt in front of him. The door swung open and Robert jumped out, his stride determined and menacing.

"Where is she, Andrew?"

"What are you doing here?"

"You can't keep me locked up, and you can't keep Sarah from me. Where is she?"

"Somewhere safe." Andrew opened his car door, intent on leaving.

Robert pushed it shut and crowded him. "Tell me where she is."

His bullying might work on Sarah, but Andrew wasn't afraid of him. "You will never see her again. I'll make sure of that."

Robert's voice lowered into a quiet hiss. "She's mine,

Andrew. She may be your sister but she's my wife. I will find her and when I do, she's coming home with me."

Robert was so close that Andrew could smell the alcohol on his breath. The man was out of control and Andrew was determined that his sister would not be a victim again. "That's never going to happen."

Robert inched back and gave a warped smile. "You'd better watch your back. You and that woman with you. One of you will tell me where my wife is."

He strutted back to his truck and roared away, but his threat loomed heavy on Andrew's mind. What lengths would Robert go to in order to get to Sarah?

The police cars parked in front of his apartment building weren't a good sign.

Andrew's gut clenched, Robert's threat still fresh on his mind. He zipped into his parking space and quickly got out.

The building manager, Mr. Wilson, met him as he approached the stairs that led to his second floor apartment.

"What happened here?" Andrew asked.

"I was about to phone you, Mr. Jennings. I saw the fellow take off so I called the police."

"What happened?"

"The guy kicked in the door. He broke in."

Andrew rushed up the stairs. His apartment door was standing open, the lock busted by apparently being kicked in. Inside, the place was trashed—furniture overturned, drawers emptied, but nothing appeared to be missing at first sight. Whoever had done this had not been there to rob him. He'd had another motive.

And Andrew was certain he knew what that motive was.

A refrigerator magnet held a photo of Sarah and Robert together, smiling. That hadn't been there before. No way would he have such a picture hanging on his refrigerator.

Mr. Wilson finally climbed the stairs and looked around. He whistled at the sight. "What a mess. Did he get much?"

Andrew pulled the photo from the magnet. "You said you saw the man who did this?"

"Yep. I got a pretty good look at him. It wasn't anybody I recognized."

Andrew handed him the photo. "Was this the man you saw?" His gut clenched as he waited for the elderly man to scan the photo.

Please don't let it be him.

Mr. Wilson slid off his glasses then nodded as he handed the photo back to Andrew. "That's the same fellow all right. You know him?"

He leaned into the sink as the weight of his landlord's words sank in. Jessica had been right, after all. This was the first place Robert had come looking for Sarah.

Had he not listened to Jessica, he might have come home to much more than a trashed apartment.

Sarah might be dead.

A jingle from the porch grabbed Jessica's attention. Her pulse quickened but she waited to act. The jingle stopped abruptly—too abruptly, as if someone's hand had quieted them.

She placed her laptop on the coffee table and moved cautiously toward the door. A shadow moved in front of the window and her breath caught. Fear prickled up her spine. Someone was out there.

Get a grip, Jessica.

She took a deep, calming breath then blew it out. She

was letting her paranoia run wild again. Whoever was there was probably only a salesman or a neighbor searching for a lost pet. Or perhaps Andrew had returned to check on her. She waited for the reassuring ring of the bell or knock on the door.

It didn't come.

Jessica moved quietly to the window and peeked through the curtains. She saw only the back of a man, tall and broad. He reached for the door handle and tried it. The rattling sent chills through Jessica.

He was trying to get into the house!

Her first instinct was to run, dash out through the back and hide, but she swallowed her fear. She would not be run out of her home like some wimpy, frightened woman who couldn't take care of herself. She wouldn't let this thug scare her away.

She reached for the light switch by the door and flipped it on, basking the porch in bright light from the freshly installed bulb. The man swore and blocked the light with his arm, hiding his face in the process, then turned and rushed from the porch, his boots clunking against the wooden planks.

Jessica pushed away from the window, fear ripping through every fiber of her at that sound. The clomping of boots on the wooden floor would be a sound that forever haunted her. She grabbed the phone then crouched beneath the desk and tried to dial 911. Her hands shook with fear and she had trouble hitting the right buttons.

She closed her eyes and took a deep calming breath. This wasn't Mitch. Mitch was in a maximum security prison two states away.

Lord, when will I be over this?

A knock on the door caused her to yelp and drop the phone.

He was back!

She peeked out from the desk toward the door, realizing Mitch would never knock.

"Jessica, it's me. Andrew Jennings."

Andrew, her rescuer!

She crawled from beneath the desk, picked up the phone and placed it back on the desk. Andrew she could deal with.

"Coming," she called, but even to her own ears her voice sounded jittery.

She opened the door to find him leaning against the jamb. He looked as pensive and worried as she felt. He brushed past her into the house and Jessica's thoughts immediately went to Sarah.

She closed the door. "What's the matter?"

He paced the floor, locking his fingers together and pressing them over his head in a gesture of worry. "You were right. I should have trusted you sooner."

Her sense of mission overrode her previous fears. Jessica reached for Andrew's arm. "Calm down and tell me what's happened."

Her touch seemed to calm him. "It's Robert. He was at my apartment. If I'd acted on my instinct…if you hadn't convinced me to have Sarah stay at the shelter…"

He couldn't finish. But he didn't need to. She already knew what might have occurred. Sarah might have been killed tonight.

A chill swept over her. This was all too coincidental not to be connected. She briefly told Andrew about the man on her porch, omitting of course the part about her hiding under the desk like a frightened little girl.

He took a deep breath as the reality of the situation hit him. "He came here too, trying to get to Sarah through you. I saw him earlier. He threatened you."

So it had been Robert who'd left that note. Robert who had been in her yard. That seemed the most likely scenario given the details. She shuddered as the sound of those boots clomping against the wooden porch replayed in her mind. She would definitely check the website again to make certain Mitch was where he was supposed to be, but for now it looked as if she had a different problem.

Robert Young was escalating, and there was no telling what he would do in order to get to Sarah.

FOUR

Jessica gripped her coffee cup with both hands, mostly to keep them from shaking. She was trying to cope, trying to maintain a strong facade, but Andrew's pacing back and forth in the kitchen of the shelter did nothing to calm her nerves.

Normally, this type of harassment wouldn't faze her, but the haunting sounds of boots against the wooden porch and the fear she'd experienced because of it left her rattled. She'd been the one to suggest coming to the shelter and Andrew had agreed. Margo had come when Jessica called about the attempted break-in.

Margo tapped her pen against the table as she studied Jessica. "So you didn't see the man's face, then?"

"No. His back was to me, but he was tall."

"Robert's tall."

Margo rolled her eyes at Andrew's comment. "So are about a million other guys." She turned back to Jessica. "How tall?"

Jessica struggled to recall the details but everything was now so muddled. It frustrated her to have those memories fading so quickly. She always cautioned women to look for the details and now she couldn't recall any herself. It was physiological. Adrenaline caused confusion. It

was often why witness testimonies were notoriously un-
reliable. She shrugged at Margo's question. "Tall enough
to set off my chimes." Logical reason began to return.
Mitch was six-foot-one so she'd positioned the chimes so
that anyone over six feet would run into them, thereby
alerting her to their presence. "Six feet at least."

"What I want to know is what he's doing out," Andrew said. "I thought he was in custody. It is still the
cops' job to lock these guys up, right?" Sarcasm dripped
from his lips.

"We do lock them up," Margo shot back. "Then you
lawyer types let them out again." She sighed. "We haven't
been able to locate him to pick him up for violating the
restraining order. He wasn't at the house when I picked
up Jessica's car."

"And you didn't bother telling us this?" He pulled a
hand through his hair and turned away. He opened one
cabinet then another. Then another.

"What are you doing?" Jessica demanded, nearing her
limit of frustration.

"Looking for a coffee mug." He turned, leaving the
bare cabinets and empty shelves exposed. "You must
have some."

Heat rose in Jessica's face at the sight of those bare
shelves, a reminder that they were short on funds and
donations for the month. "Try the dishwasher."

He opened the dishwasher and jerked on the top rack,
pulling it too hard too fast. The rack lost its wheel and
Andrew had to grab it to keep it from falling.

Jessica rushed over. "Be careful! You're going to break
it." She pushed him aside and fixed it herself then handed
him a mug.

"Looks like it doesn't work too well, anyway." He
walked to the sink and rinsed out his cup.

Jessica fumed at his haughty attitude. There he went again, diminishing her life's work. Gone was the cama- raderie she'd felt with him earlier.

Margo interrupted before Jessica laid into him.

"I'll file a report but I think you both know the drill. You can't prove it was Robert on your porch so there is really nothing the police can do at this point. The one bright spot I see in this is that he may still not know where the shelter is located."

Jessica knew the truth. "It won't take him long to find us."

"Probably not. But I wouldn't make it easy for him. I recommend you stay here for a few days and keep the place on lockdown."

Andrew nodded. "That's a good idea. You're too easy a target at home."

Jessica stared at them both, dumbfounded by the idea that everyone expected her to run and hide…and that she had to keep repeating herself. "How many times do I have to say this? I won't be run out of my home by someone like Robert Young."

"I'm only suggesting you take precautions. You've stayed at the shelter lots of times."

"Sure, but that's by choice." She folded her arms and stood her ground. "You're suggesting I hide out."

"Well, what's wrong with that? You're practically here all the time, anyway."

"But don't you see? It's my choice, Margo. I won't let one of these psychos control my life." She'd already given Mitch enough control over her life. She wouldn't allow it to happen again.

Condescending annoyance dripped from Andrew's words. "Need I remind you that Robert nearly killed you yesterday?"

She mocked his snotty phrase. "You needn't remind me of anything." How had she ever thought Andrew Jennings was on her side?

"What if he gets into the house? What are you going to do then, Jessica? Cower under the desk hoping he'll go away?"

Her heart jumped. How had he known she'd cowered under the desk? He couldn't know that. "Pardon me?"

"This guy has already scared you half to death and all he did was get onto the porch and rattle a door handle. What are you going to do when he gets inside?"

Her ire went on high alert. How dare he suggest she'd been afraid? "I was not scared."

He closed the distance between them as if his closeness would act as a reminder. "You were trembling when you answered the door and your heart was racing."

"It was not."

"Was, too."

Jessica stared him in the eye. "First of all, you couldn't possibly know whether or not my heart was racing and second, if I seemed frightened, it was only because I was responding to the fear I heard in your voice."

He studied her then shook his head in disbelief. "Wow. Are you really that stubborn that you won't even admit when you're afraid? You sound just like them."

"Who?"

"These women you counsel. I'll tell you the truth, Jessica. Right now, you remind me a lot of my sister. She didn't know when to play it smart, either."

She clenched her hands into fists. She wanted nothing more than to smack that arrogant attitude right out of him and demand he leave her shelter. She'd run off bigger and meaner men than Andrew Jennings before.

But she didn't. Instead, she turned and walked away,

marching into her office and closing the door. She didn't need to sit and listen to Andrew give her an account of her behavior.

She grabbed a manual—it didn't matter which one—and sat at her desk, but minutes later when Margo peeked inside, Jessica was still staring at page one.

Margo closed the door behind her. "Don't worry. Mr. Tall, Dark and Annoying is gone."

"Good."

Instead of choosing a chair, Margo hopped onto the edge of the desk. "Is he right, Jess?"

She cringed. "You know I hate that nickname, Margo."

She nodded. "I know terror flashes across your face when I say it."

"Then why do you?"

"Because I keep hoping one day it won't be so pronounced, but it's always the same—sheer terror at the mention of a name."

Jessica didn't know how to respond. She knew Margo wanted her to open up and share, confide with her friend about what she'd endured, but she couldn't. Talking about her ordeal with Mitch only weakened her.

"You counsel all these women to share their experiences, yet you continue to keep yours hidden, bottled up so tightly that you think no one notices." She stood. "We notice, honey. Believe me, you can't hide that kind of pain forever."

Jessica leaned back in her chair. Margo was her best friend and knew her better than anyone else. She might be right. In fact, she probably was right, but Jessica knew she wouldn't be able to function if she opened up about Mitch. She had to remain calm and in control if she hoped to help others survive what she'd been through.

Trouble was her control was slowly but surely slipping away.

"It might not have been Robert who was on my porch," she admitted. "In fact, it probably wasn't. There's no reason to believe he knows where I live."

"That's true."

"It could have been anyone."

Margo nodded. "Maybe, but we can't discount Robert Young. He is dangerous."

Jessica nodded, but she already felt better convincing herself that she'd blown the entire incident out of proportion.

Mitch was still in prison, safely locked away where he could never reach her again.

And Robert Young she could handle.

Andrew wanted to check on his sister one more time before he left. He would never forget the terror he'd felt at finding his apartment trashed and the realization that Sarah could have been killed had she been there, had Andrew trusted his own instincts instead of listening to Jessica's.

He found Sarah in the common area rocking and singing to one of the babies residing at the shelter with her mother. Andrew watched her with that baby. She was a natural. She'd always been the nurturing one, and his heart longed to see her settled and safe with a good husband and a family of her own.

He gave her a little wave when she spotted him over the baby's head. She was safe and that was all that mattered to him now. And, as much as it pained him to admit, it wasn't because of him. He hadn't been able to protect her. Jessica had been right to push him. He understood that now and was glad his pig-headedness hadn't gotten his sister killed.

He made his way back to the grocery store, realizing he hadn't eaten for hours. As he waited in line, he noticed a little girl in a shopping cart waving to him. He smiled and waved back, causing her to giggle. He watched the girl's mother poking and prodding the produce for the freshest choice. She picked up a bag of grapes causing the little girl to clap. But when she noticed the price she put them back and Andrew overheard her tell the girl they were too expensive.

The deli server drew his attention, and he placed his order. When he looked again, the little girl and her mother were gone. But the brief encounter had sent his mind back to the baby at the shelter, the one Sarah had been rocking. The common room was sparsely furnished and the play area for the children had only a few toys. And the practically bare cupboards... He knew the center operated on donations, and it seemed to him funds must be meager.

The lady behind the counter called to him and he accepted his food and quickly scanned his credit card. He was signing his name when it hit him. He couldn't swing a hammer to save his life and he didn't know how to fix that old dishwasher or do any of the repairs the shelter needed, but he did make a good living. He could afford to offer something to the shelter, especially since his own sister was living there now.

He stopped himself before he made any more excuses. This had nothing to do with his sister. Sarah would never go hungry or homeless as long as he could help it. He wanted to help the shelter because of Jessica, because she fought through fear and stood up for those she guarded. He admired that. He'd seen the look of terror on her face and he'd felt her pulse racing when she'd grabbed his arm. She had tenacity and he liked that.

He hated to admit it. Despite how crazy she made him, he admired her.

He asked to see the manager then made arrangements to have groceries sent to the shelter. He also bought a bag of seedless grapes and tracked down the little girl in the cart.

Tonight, no child would go without, not on his watch.

The dark house mocked her. She should have stayed at the shelter tonight, but her pride wouldn't allow it. She would not be run out of her own home by fear.

Jessica quickly got out of the car and rushed toward the front door. The hairs on her neck prickled with fear. Her gaze spread over the lawn, the street and the neighbors' houses. Everything looked normal. Nothing seemed odd or out of place. She let herself into the house. Nothing looked out of place either, but she couldn't shake the feeling that something wasn't right. She deposited her purse on the desk then opened her laptop and powered it up, navigating quickly to the Dover County Correctional Facility website. She typed in the inmate number she knew by heart and watched as the page loaded. A photograph of Mitch appeared on the screen. She no longer saw the handsome sharp features or the piercing eyes that had first attracted her to Mitch Reynolds. Now, when she looked at him, all she saw was the monster. He'd replaced expensive suits with an orange jumpsuit and a two-hundred-dollar hairstyle with a buzz cut. She breathed a deep sigh of relief when she saw his status hadn't changed. He was still locked up serving a life sentence for murder.

She hadn't really believed it was him, but the echoing

sound of those boots against her floor had brought back
memories she'd tried so hard to bury. She shuddered as
they flowed back to her. Margo was right. She needed
to talk to someone about him. She needed to be free of
his control once and for all.

She stared at his face again and shivered with fear.
Even in the photograph, his eyes seemed to whisper to
her.

You're mine, Jess.

She closed the computer. Maybe she would work on
her issues with Mitch tomorrow.

Instead, she turned her mind to more practical matters, shelter matters. Dean's Den ran mostly on donations, and lately they hadn't been coming in. She fixed
herself a glass of warm milk then kicked off her shoes
and curled up on the sofa with her Bible and a blanket.
She would pray about keeping this house. The small sal-
ary she earned from doing crisis intervention calls for the
county wasn't much, but it had provided her the means
to have her own place. She didn't want to do anything to
jeopardize the shelter, but she did enjoy having a place
to get away to. But maybe that was the point. Maybe
she wasn't supposed to get away. The other women who
stayed there had nowhere to go. Why should she?

Most of the women at the shelter knew poverty. Jessica had hoped to protect them from that kind of life at
least for a little while. No one should have to worry about
where their next meal would come from when bigger issues like physical safety were a major concern. She'd
taken them in and promised them shelter and protection
and three meals a day. So far, with God's help and generous donations, she'd been able to keep those promises.
But this time she was very close to failing them.

She cringed remembering the bare cabinets Andrew

had examined and left standing open, revealing their empty shelves. She opened her Bible and prayed for God to speak His wisdom to her. Resentment was already settling into her heart, resentment at people like Andrew Jennings who never had to worry about where they would get money for their next meal. Sarah was not her typical client. Jessica remembered Andrew's fierce protectiveness, and jealousy twinged at her but also admiration. How could she not admire him? He took care of his sister in the same way Jessica took care of the women in her care.

God, please help us. These women and children need to eat, and come tomorrow I'll have nothing to feed them. We need Your intervention.

"We're so glad you came by." Olivia loaded another heap of mashed potatoes onto Andrew's plate then placed a kiss on the top of his head. "We've missed you."

He'd phoned Tom after leaving the grocery store and was told to come right over. Spending the evening visiting with Tom and Olivia was the smartest decision he'd made in a long time.

"I've missed you guys, too. It's been too long."

"So what have you been up to lately, Andrew? Besides getting your face on television all the time?"

"Working mostly."

"What about church? Are you attending anywhere?"

"No. I haven't set foot in church since…"

She nodded, seeming to understand. "Tory's funeral."

He set down his fork and sighed. He'd known this would come up eventually. Tory and Olivia had been best friends since college. "Yes."

"You know I still find myself picking up the phone

to call her or wondering why she hasn't called me even after all this time."

He knew that feeling. Expecting to see her when he walked into the apartment. Expecting to hear her on his voice mail. His jaw tightened as he pushed back those memories.

"How's your family doing?" Tom asked, changing the subject away from Tory. Olivia seemed a little disheartened, but Andrew was glad for the change in subject.

"My mom's living in Florida with her cousin. I talk to her every week, but I haven't really seen her since the first of the year."

"And Sarah?"

"She's here. She's had some trouble recently." He explained the situation to them. "She's staying at a local shelter."

"Olivia used to do volunteer work at a local domestic violence shelter—Dean's Den."

"That's where Sarah is. So you know Jessica, then?"

Olivia nodded. "Sure. I've helped her out with some tax issues in the past."

He knew he was walking into a landmine of questions, but he just had to ask. "What do you think about her?"

"Jessica? She's great. She's passionate, determined—"

"Reckless?"

She shook her head, a bewildered look on her face. "I don't know what you mean."

"The thing is I've watched her take some risks, and I'm sure they weren't necessary."

"She deals with dangerous situations sometimes."

Tom finally interjected. "I don't mean to overstep here, Andrew, but is this about Jessica...or Tory?"

"This has nothing to do with Tory."

"Doesn't it? You often complained that Tory took too many unnecessary risks."

"That's completely different. Tory worked in an office. Jessica's entire life is one big risk."

"Are you worried about Sarah's safety?"

"No. I've been to the shelter and I've seen the security measures. Sarah's fine."

Olivia exchanged a glance with her husband. "So then it's Jessica you're worried about?" The knowing smile she tried to hide told Andrew he'd given them the wrong idea.

"Robert is dangerous. He'll do anything to try to get to Sarah. I just don't want to see anything happen to Jessica because she helped us."

Olivia covered Andrew's hand with her own in a reassuring gesture. "Jessica can take care of herself. I've seen her stand up to people and situations that would send me scampering for cover."

"I'm sure you're right. I don't know why I worry like I do."

"Because you're a kind man, Andrew, and you care about those around you."

"Besides," Tom interjected, "I'm sure nothing is going to happen."

Andrew hoped his friends were right. Being here with them did help him feel better and he was glad he'd come. But before he could tell them so, footfalls in the hallway grabbed all their attention. Two little girls came running and squealing down the hall and into the dining room. He scooped them up and hugged them both tight, pulling them into his lap. Olivia laughed and got up, walking over to Tom and wrapping her arms around his neck.

Andrew watched the scene unfold and felt a pang of sorrow pierce him. Yet he was surprised to realize it wasn't Tory he missed as much as the dreams he'd had for them.

* * *

The shrill ring of her cell phone jerked Jessica from a sound sleep. She grabbed for the phone, realizing she'd fallen asleep on the couch. Her Bible still lay across her chest and the glass of milk was still full.

"Jessica, you'll never believe this." Mia's voice was rushed and excited. "We just received a delivery from Vowell's Market. They said it was an anonymous donation. It looks like we are fully stocked on groceries now."

Relief flowed through her followed by a realization of how good God was. She'd just been praying about this very thing last night and already God's hand had provided for them.

"Some of the women are planning a big breakfast. Come join us."

"I'm on my way."

Jessica pushed back the blanket and got up. Excitement rushed through her as she dressed. God always had a way of working things out. Why did she ever doubt Him?

She thought of Andrew and the fierce protectiveness he had for his sister that reminded her so much of Dean. Was it possible God felt that same fierce protectiveness? And He had the means to really safeguard them. It was exciting to watch His hand at work in her ministry.

Still, she allowed herself a moment of gloating. She only hoped Andrew stopped by today so he could see for himself how well she provided for those in her care.

She felt herself flush as she realized that wasn't the only reason she hoped Andrew would come around today. Despite the blowout they'd had yesterday at the shelter, she couldn't deny her sudden attachment to him or the growing hope that the attraction might be mutual. Was it possible something could grow between her and Andrew?

She sighed, realizing that was an impossible dream.

Andrew had said she was just like the women she counseled…and he was right. She was one of them. And men like Andrew—men who had high-powered women lawyers and fashion models throwing themselves at him—would never settle for someone like her.

"She's made bad choices," Andrew had said of Sarah's dilemma. What would he say if he discovered how much her bad choices had cost Dean?

She shook her head, trying to clear out any thoughts of a future between her and Andrew. It was ridiculous to even contemplate.

She turned on the coffeemaker, anxious to get moving and get to the shelter to see the provisions for herself.

She rushed into the bedroom to get dressed but stopped when she turned toward her dresser. The same words from the note were scrawled in what appeared to be lipstick on her mirror.

You can't stop true love!

Suddenly, the weight of the truth barreled down on her. Robert had been inside the house, might possibly still be inside.

Jessica screamed and ran.

Andrew had just parked outside Jessica's house when he heard the scream. He dropped the box of donuts he'd picked up as a peace offering and ran toward the porch. The front door flew open and Jessica ran from the house, barefoot and without a coat, ignoring the shrill of the alarm and the wail of the wind chimes as she rushed past them.

"Jessica!" He rushed to her and she ran into his arms without hesitation.

Her body shook with fear, tears streaming down her face. "He—he was in my house."

He pushed hair back from her face then slipped out of his jacket and draped it over her shoulders. "Wait here."

Andrew started toward the house but Jessica grabbed his arm. "No! What if he's still inside?"

"If he is then I want to make sure he doesn't get away." He pushed his cell phone into her hand. "Call 911. Tell them you've had a break-in."

He hopped up onto the porch and moved cautiously toward the door. He scanned the living room, noticing the full glass of milk and open Bible and blanket on the couch. The aroma of coffee filled the house but nothing seemed out of place.

He saw the writing as he entered the bedroom. Robert had been in the house, possibly while Jessica had slept. He could have gotten to her at any moment.

Anger ripped through him. He wouldn't let Robert hurt anyone else he cared about.

He retreated from the house so he didn't contaminate the scene. He wanted all the evidence possible to convict Robert of breaking into Jessica's house and terrorizing her.

Outside, Andrew pulled Jessica against him, and she didn't protest. She wrapped her arms around his waist and rested her head against his shoulder without hesitation, and it felt as if she belonged there, nestled against him.

When the police arrived, he was by her side as she answered questions about the break-in. "So you didn't actually see anyone inside the house?" the officer asked.

Her voice was still shaky when she answered. "No, but he was there. It was the same message that was on the note I found on my car yesterday."

"We'll check it out." He motioned to his partner and together they entered the house.

Andrew led her to his car and opened the passenger

door so she could sit down. "I'll go inside and ask about getting your shoes and maybe a cup of coffee." She nodded her agreement and he dashed into the house and okayed the items with the officer.

"We've contacted officers to come and photograph the scene and dust for prints. After that, your girlfriend can come back in."

He started to correct the officer about Jessica being his girlfriend but stopped before the words came as another comment the officer made grabbed his attention—the one about Jessica returning to the house. She wouldn't really consider coming back here to stay…would she?

Not after this fright. Not after Robert had gotten inside.

He took her a hot cup of coffee, her tennis shoes and her coat he'd found hung over the back of a kitchen chair. She might not need the coat once the sun broke through the haze of the morning fog, but for now the morning air was chilly. She slipped into her shoes and the coat and took the coffee with a grateful thank-you.

Andrew knelt beside her and studied her as a flurry of activity began around them when additional police cars and the crime scene van arrived. She looked so vulnerable at the moment, but what would happen when the shock and fear wore off? Would she revert to her stubborn stance, or had this encounter finally helped her see reason? He couldn't take that chance.

He had to act now, before the shock wore off, if he wanted to convince her that remaining here was dangerous. "I know you don't want to hear this, Jessica, but I don't think it's safe for you to stay here any longer. Think about the women at the shelter. They need you. You can't risk their lives by risking your own."

He expected a backlash, a flash of anger to light up

her face and a quick rebuke about minding his own business, but she nodded instead of protesting. "I think you're right."

Was there any clearer sign that she was afraid? "I'll ask if you can go inside to pack a bag."

"Andrew." He turned back to look at her. "I won't tell him where Sarah is. No matter what he does, I won't ever tell him."

"It never crossed my mind you might," he told her and that was the truth. He'd seen more sides to Jessica in the past two days than he'd seen in all the time he'd known her, and the amazing thing was he was impressed with this woman more than he'd ever thought he would be.

Once the police gave the all-clear, Jessica reentered her house. Andrew was by her side as he had been all morning, sitting next to her, comforting her, bringing her donuts he'd salvaged from the box he'd dropped in the yard earlier.

From the moment she stepped back into her home, she knew it was tainted. She shuddered, realizing she couldn't stay here anymore. She didn't want to stay here anymore. Like the women she counseled, her home had become a place of fear and uncertainty. She'd prayed for a sign from God about whether or not to keep her little house. She'd gotten her sign. It was time to let it go.

She headed for her bedroom and Andrew helped pull down her suitcase from the top shelf of the closet. They both purposefully avoided looking at the mirror as she stuffed clothes into her bags. How many times had she been on the other side of this task, pressuring someone to pack hurriedly to avoid any potential danger? Well, no one had to pressure her. The red smears on her mirror took care of that.

She grabbed her makeup from the top of the dresser and tossed it into her makeup bag, realizing as she did that her lipstick container was missing. She glanced up at the writing—her shade of red, no doubt.

She closed her suitcase then grabbed her computer and her photograph of Dean and followed Andrew as he carried her suitcase to her car.

As she reached the porch steps, a scampering underneath startled her. She jumped, stumbling down the steps. Andrew dropped the suitcase and caught her, his muscles tightening against her.

Her heart pounded against her chest as she glanced at the bottom of her porch. "What was that?"

She'd once counseled a lady whose boyfriend had hidden under the house until the police left, then broke inside and raped her. Had Robert done that? Had he been hiding under the house the entire time the police were searching for him?

Andrew slid his finger to his lips, motioning for her to keep silent. He knelt down and peered under the porch. Jessica grabbed her cell phone, ready to dial 911 again.

But Andrew's posture relaxed and he smiled up at her. "Looks like you've got a squatter all right, but I don't think he's any threat." He reached for whatever was beneath the porch and Jessica heard the yapping of Mrs. Brady's dog as he pulled him out by the collar.

"What are you doing under there?" she asked the pup. "Mrs. Brady never lets him wander free."

He squirmed and yapped in Andrew's arms, trying to get loose again.

"What's the matter, boy? You know me." She looked at Andrew. "I'm sure Mrs. Brady doesn't know he's out. I'd better return him."

She crossed the yard, heading toward Mrs. Brady's

home. It wasn't like her to let Marlon out of her sight. But as Jessica approached the house, she noticed a place in the fence where it looked as if Marlon had dug his way out.

She glanced back at the little dog who'd settled down in Andrew's arms. "Did you do that? Did you dig your way under the fence?"

Marlon yapped a response.

"Hello, Jessica!"

She turned and spotted her neighbor heading toward them. "Hello, Mr. Percy."

"I saw the police cars earlier. Did something happen?"

"Someone broke into my house so I'll be staying at the shelter for a while."

He nodded. "That's probably a smart idea. Young ladies can't be too careful these days." He spotted the dog in Andrew's hands. "I see Marlon escaped."

"Yes, he was hiding under my porch. Mr. Percy, this is Andrew Jennings, a friend of mine."

Andrew reached out and shook hands with the older man.

"I'll take him," he said taking hold of the pup. "He probably misses his mama. I suppose you heard about Mrs. Brady."

"What do you mean?"

"She fell yesterday and broke her hip. It's a shame, really. She was so active. Her nephew is in from out of town taking care of things while she's in the hospital. I met him yesterday."

So that was why Marlon was on the loose. "I had no idea." Jessica hated to hear something bad had happened to her neighbor. She wasn't aware Mrs. Brady had any relatives other than the sister she'd mentioned, but it was a blessing she had family to care for her.

"He seemed like a nice young fellow, the nephew. Big

guy, very charming and sure of himself. He reminded me of one of those slick used-car salesmen."

Jessica knew the type. She knew it too well. How many times had she heard that description of Mitch? No one could believe such a handsome face could house the monster beneath.

"I'll have to go by and visit her."

"I'm sure she'd like that. Take care, Jessica, and it was nice to meet you, Andrew."

"I'm sorry something happened to your friend," Andrew said as Mr. Percy walked away with Marlon, who went into a frenzied yapping fit. "She seemed very nice."

"Yes, she is a very nice lady."

"It's good that she has family to look out for her. Everyone should have that." Andrew reached for her hand and held it.

Jessica was surprised at how much she enjoyed the feel of his strong hands surrounding hers, but his comment struck her. He must have been referring to Sarah, but she was reminded of Dean, and how she'd let him down. Why did everything have to remind her that she would never be free of her past? She was happy Andrew had been here for her today, and she would love to have more days with him around, but what chance would they have if he knew the truth about how Dean died?

She held tightly to his hand, taking comfort in his presence while she still could.

FIVE

A plea agreement in the Trevino case left Andrew with his morning unexpectedly open. He returned to his office, tossed his suit jacket across the chair and tried to concentrate on what he needed to do next. He had other cases that required his attention, but today all his thoughts were centered on Jessica and the sudden, unexpected—and pleasant—change in their relationship.

Last week, she'd been that annoying voice second-guessing his decision on domestic disturbance cases. This week, she was the woman whose touch had scrambled his ability for coherent thought. He focused on a photo of Tory on his desk. When had his attention shifted from her to Jessica? And why did it not bother him that it had?

He picked up the phone to dial Jessica's number. He wanted to check on her, to make certain Robert hadn't made another appearance.

He also wanted to hear the warmth of her voice.

A knock on his door stopped him before he finished dialing. Leslie poked her head into his office. "Bill heard you were back. He wants to see you in the conference room."

Andrew hung up the phone. "Do you know why?"

"No idea, but CJ is with him."

Andrew frowned but got up and headed down the hall toward the conference room. As he opened the door, he spotted Robert sitting with another man on one side of the massive table. Bill and CJ were positioned on the opposite side.

Bill waved him inside. "Come in, Andrew. I believe you know everyone except possibly Mr. David Carlisle, your brother-in-law's attorney."

"What are they doing here?"

Mr. Carlisle stood. "On behalf of my client, I want to inform you that we will be filing formal charges against you and this office for misuse of authority."

"What are you talking about? What misuse of authority?"

"You assaulted my client during the abduction of his wife from her home."

Anger pulsed through him. "I rescued her from that prison."

"That will be for the bar association to decide."

He ran a hand through his hair and glared at Robert. "You go right ahead and try these lame attempts to get to me, but you will never get to Sarah from behind bars."

Bill cleared his throat. "That's another reason I asked you in here. We won't be pursuing a case against Mr. Young."

He turned to Bill, dumbfounded. "Why not?"

CJ spoke up, her tone chiding him. "You tainted our case by assaulting the man."

"I was protecting my sister."

Bill interrupted their tiff. "The restraining order will still be in place for your sister's safety."

Mr. Carlisle stood. "I think we're done here." He motioned for Robert, who stopped beside Andrew and flashed him a smug smile before walking out.

When he was gone, Andrew turned to Bill. "How could you do that? That man is a monster."

CJ responded. "You're an officer of the court, Andrew. Don't think the defense wouldn't use that to insinuate harassment in any case we bring against him that you're involved in. Carlisle was practically drooling to drag this office through the ringer for your behavior."

"What about my sister's safety? He's already violated the restraining order."

"Next time, have her call the police instead of you."

"Enough, CJ." Bill turned to Andrew. "The District Attorney's office cannot afford to be involved in a scandal. Imagine how that would affect our authority. All of your cases, past and present, would be tainted."

"He's dangerous, Bill. He needs to be locked up. He's terrorized my sister for months plus he trashed my apartment. He's been harassing Jessica for information about Sarah's location and there's no telling what lengths he'll go to to find her. Does he have to make good on his threats to kill us all before this office will step up and put him away?"

"We go after the cases we can win," CJ reminded him.

"Look, Andrew, I feel for you. I really do, but we've been through this. We had no choice but to drop the previous charges because your sister wouldn't substantiate them. Now this assault is tainted, as well. I'm sorry, but our hands are tied in this matter."

"We have to do something to get him off the streets before he kills someone."

"Legally, we have no recourse."

Andrew stormed out and headed back to his office. He slammed the door and paced in front of it. It wasn't fair. Robert was going to get away with beating and terrorizing his sister and there was nothing he could do about it.

He sat in his chair and took a deep breath, trying to calm down. As he glanced up, he noticed a box on top of his filing cabinet. He knew what was inside that box. He pulled it to him. He'd ordered the file from storage after Margo shoved the case into his face. He'd been hoping to justify himself and his case, but he'd never opened it, never reviewed it.

He knew why.

He opened it now and read through the evidence. Things kept popping out at him, things he'd refused to see. Threats he'd insisted were inadmissible. Medical records he hadn't fought hard enough to include in order to establish a pattern of abuse. He should have done more to protect this woman from her husband, but instead he'd focused his case on the assault against the innocent bystander. It was a quicker and easier win. At least it had seemed so at the time.

He unfolded the newspaper he'd stuck in the file. The headline screamed at him about the slaughter Tim Meadows had inflicted on his family only two months after his release. The D.A.'s office, and Andrew particularly, had received a lot of criticism for not stopping this madman, for not protecting the innocent. Maybe he couldn't have won the case, but he should have tried harder.

But he knew something most of the general public didn't understand. His job wasn't to protect. It was to prosecute.

Sarah was no better off. The law was not going to protect her from Robert. They would merely be there to pick up the pieces once he made good on his threat. Now she had only him for protection, him and Jessica.

He closed the file and pushed it away, realizing that

Jessica had been right about him. He'd had an attitude that downgraded domestic violence… That is until it had hit him personally.

Andrew stood as Jessica entered the café and spotted him.

"Thanks for coming," he said as she approached the table.

"I'm glad you called." She ordered an iced tea with lemon from the waitress who delivered his drink, then slid out of her jacket and hung it across the back of her chair.

"What's going on? You sounded upset on the phone."

He sat down. "I just found out the D.A.'s office isn't going to pursue charges against Robert."

"Why?"

"Bill and CJ seem to think I contaminated the case when I hit him."

She shook her head. "Ridiculous."

"Now he'll think he's invincible. There's no telling what he'll do to get to Sarah."

He was right. The threat Robert posed to Sarah had just increased. They needed to take more drastic measures to protect her. "I'll call around to find a safe house for her where she can stay."

"It's not just Sarah I'm concerned about." He reached across the table and touched her hand. "You need to think about your safety, too."

She turned her hand and locked fingers with him, enjoying the idea that he was worried about her. "I'm already staying at the shelter full-time. I routinely double-check the safety measures. I don't know what else I can do. The fact of the matter is that if someone is really in-

tent on getting inside, there are always ways. That's why
I recommend sending Sarah to a safe house."

"You didn't see his face today. He was so smug. He
doesn't think anyone can touch him. You're in danger,
too. I don't want you to go out alone. Don't go to the
store, don't go to the courthouse, don't go anywhere unless someone is with you."

She hesitated. Precautions were one thing but he was
talking about being on full lockdown. Her initial response
was to refuse. She'd already given up so much because
of Robert Young. Could she really allow him to take
more? "That's a lot to ask. I still have to do my job." But
as she remembered the malice she'd seen in his face,
she knew they'd only glimpsed what this man was capable of. She shuddered, thinking of the words smeared
across her mirror.

"My trial has ended so I'll have some free time. Please
promise me you won't go out by yourself. I'm worried
about your safety."

She smiled at the idea of having Andrew around more.
But that would only put his life at risk. "You need to take
precautions, too, Andrew."

"Don't worry about me. I can take care of myself."

"How would Sarah feel if something happened to you?
If Robert harmed you?"

She pulled her hand away from his and stirred the
ice in her tea. He needed to know what could happen to
him…but was she ready to share this story? She looked
into the determined set of his face and knew she had to.
He needed to understand the danger.

"I once knew this woman who got mixed up with the
wrong man. She thought she was in love, but her dream
man turned violent. He threatened to kill her if she tried
to leave him. She asked her brother for help."

"Sounds like me and Sarah."

"Yes, it does."

"What happened to her? Did she get away from him?"

Jessica closed her eyes, reliving that awful night in one moment. "Her abuser broke into the house intent on killing her. The brother got between them, so the man stabbed him to death instead. She was devastated. Her life was ruined. Her abuser went to jail, but she was left with nothing but guilt over what she'd done to her brother."

"She didn't do anything. It wasn't her fault her brother died."

"Wasn't it? She's the one who got involved with this man in the first place. She got him killed."

"Do you really think Robert is that dangerous?"

She gingerly touched the goose egg she still had from their last encounter. She'd seen the look of evil in his eyes. "I think he could be. And I think it's a shame the District Attorney's office doesn't recognize that danger."

"From a prosecutorial standpoint, it doesn't pose the same threat to the community as stranger assaults do."

A fire in her eye ignited on the subject of her life's work. "Are you aware domestic violence is the leading cause of injury to women—more than car accidents, muggings and rapes combined? And that the chances of being raped or robbed or murdered are more likely to occur by someone the victim knows and is usually intimate with?"

"You don't have to dictate facts to me, Jessica. I know them."

"Do you? Because you seem to be defending the status quo…the one that says Sarah is less than a victim because her attacker is her husband."

"I don't believe that."

"I hope not. If one good thing could come from this nightmare, I hope it's that you empathize more with victims than you used to, that you understand more readily what they're going through."

"I guess I do."

She covered his hand with hers again and smiled. "That's a good start, Counselor."

This is better, Jessica decided, as she settled into her office's sofa bed for the evening. She'd already checked to make sure the doors were locked and the alarm was set. Now that she would be staying at the shelter fulltime, she made a mental note to call Mr. Grayson tomorrow and let him know she would be moving out. It meant breaking her lease, but Mr. Grayson knew her situation and he would understand her taking such precautions. She would also need to set aside one of the rooms at the shelter for her own personal space. She couldn't sleep in her office long-term.

A beep alerted her to a text message on her phone. She picked it up and smiled, seeing it was from Andrew checking on her.

See you tomorrow his message stated.

She had errands to run in the morning—going to the bank, the post office, the dollar store—and Andrew had insisted on accompanying her. She should have been offended and claimed she didn't need a babysitter, but she had to admit she was glad to have his company. She did feel safer having him around, yet she doubted she would have that feeling with just anyone for company.

She responded to his text then set down her phone and got ready for bed, already looking forward to tomorrow. Who knew such mundane tasks would bring her such enjoyment? She smiled, feeling very satisfied and hopeful for the first time in a long time. Andrew Jennings had become a nice surprise.

Her phone beeped again and she relished the idea of another message from him. But when she picked up the phone, her heart fell. This message wasn't from Andrew but a number she didn't recognize. A photo of her and Andrew on her porch when he'd embraced her appeared with the caption, You can't stop true love. She shuddered at the image. That was how close he'd gotten, close enough to snap a picture of them together on her porch.

Robert knew where she lived and he'd been there watching her. She was glad now that she'd decided not to stay. Who knew what he would have done once Andrew left?

She studied the picture, recognizing the tree that separate her and Mrs. Brady's yards. She realized this picture had been taken from Mrs. Brady's. That was the only explanation. She shuddered, remembering how Marlon had been roaming free. Mrs. Brady would never allow that, but Mrs. Brady hadn't been there. She'd fallen and broken her hip.

Had Robert taken advantage of her absence to spy on her? But how had he known Mrs. Brady wouldn't be there unless… Jessica shuddered. Would Robert really stoop to battering an old woman?

Jessica was certain of it.

Had Mrs. Brady reported an assault to the police? Margo hadn't mentioned it to her. Was it possible Mrs. Brady was unable to tell anyone what had happened? Mr. Percy said she'd broken her hip, but he hadn't mentioned any head trauma. Was the woman too terrified to speak up?

Jessica made up her mind to go see her neighbor tomorrow. And if Robert was responsible for her fall then Heaven help him.

Her phone rang. She braced herself. Was Robert calling to taunt her now? She checked the caller ID and saw Margo's name and number. A sigh of relief flooded her. "Hey, Margo. What's going on? It's late."

"Are you busy?"

Jessica recognized the serious tone of Margo's voice when she answered her call. She wasn't calling just to chat at this time of night. "What do you have?"

"Amy Vance. Twenty-two years old and a college student. Her professor boyfriend attacked her with a baseball bat."

Jessica sighed. She never got used to hearing about the violence some men were capable of. "Where are you?"

She jotted down the address Margo gave her. She liked to be at the scene before the paramedics transported the victim to the hospital. The sooner Jessica arrived, the better things usually went. She phoned Mia and asked her to come in. Someone needed to be in charge while she was out in case an emergency occurred while she was gone.

It was only as she was pulling on her jacket that she remembered her promise to Andrew not to go out alone. She glanced at the clock. She would lose a half hour waiting on him to arrive. Those were precious minutes she would lose counseling Amy Vance.

She saw headlights in the parking lot and knew Mia had arrived. She couldn't wait for Andrew, and the less he knew about this the better. He might not understand, but this was her job, her mission, to help women in trouble.

She couldn't wait for an escort.

Jessica met Mia in the parking lot. "Thanks for doing this, Mia. I know it's not fair."

"It's no problem. My plans with John fell through, anyway."

"Who is John?"

Mia's face lit up. "We met at the grocery store. He has dark hair and he's tall and he wears these cowboy boots." She sighed. "He's so dreamy."

"He sounds nice."

"He is, but..." She twisted her hands nervously. "With everything I've witnessed the past few months I some-times wonder how I could ever make a relationship work. I've seen how men can be so mean. How do you get past that and trust that someone is who he says he is?"

Jessica hesitated. Who was she to offer advice on love? She was far too jaded. "I understand your concerns, but I'm not sure I'm the right person to ask about that kind of thing. It's been a very long time since I've been in a relationship."

Mia took her hand. "I really admire what you do, Jes-sica. Thank you for the opportunity to work with you."

Jessica slid into her car. She was grateful for the kind words, but Mia had gotten her thinking. Was she des-tined to be alone forever? Would she ever have another chance at love?

She smiled as Andrew's smile came to her mind. He was the first man who had caught her attention in a long, long while. Was it possible she was ready for something more than a guilt-stricken life alone?

She shuddered. She'd seen so much violence. She knew the evil of men better than anyone else.

Unable to push away the weary thoughts about her past, Jessica rolled down the window and called out to Mia. "Just be careful, Mia."

As she drove, she prepared herself mentally for what

was to come. Another violent man, another violent incident. One more battered life. It broke her heart.

The address Margo had given her was across town. She didn't usually like to take the interstate but knew it was the fastest way. Traffic was especially heavy for a Thursday night so she sped up as she approached to match their speed. Suddenly, the car behind her sped up too and swerved into the lane, essentially blocking Jessica's path and preventing her from merging. Someone was in a big hurry. The on ramp lane was ending so she slowed down to let the car pass. Instead, it slowed as well, again blocking her way and leaving her little choice but to cut the car off as she merged into traffic.

The blare of his horn sounded, but Jessica tried not to let it ruffle her.

Her phone buzzed and Jessica reached to answer it.

"Where are you?" Margo demanded.

"I'm ten minutes away."

"You might as well turn around. The paramedics are transporting our victim to the hospital. She's got a broken arm, but it could be worse."

"I'll meet you at the hospital." The hospital was in the opposite direction. She needed to get off at the next exit and turn around. She changed lanes, getting over as far as possible as quickly as possible.

The maroon car behind her did the same.

She gripped the steering wheel. That was odd. It was the same car that she'd cut off getting onto the interstate. Was it possible he was following her, waiting for her to stop so he could have words with her about her driving? She'd heard about people doing that. The news called it road rage.

Great, that was just what she needed…another enraged person threatening her.

Her mind quickly went on alert. Maybe she wasn't dealing with road rage. Maybe it was just good old plain rage she was used to. She glanced at the car in the rear-view mirror. She couldn't see much with the glare of headlights. But she remembered it from before. A maroon four-door sedan. Her mind immediately went to Robert. Was it possible he was following her now, waiting for her to stop, waiting for his moment to strike? But he drove a white truck, not a maroon sedan. Of course, what would stop him from borrowing a car or even stealing one?

Nothing.

She swerved back into another lane secretly hoping she was only being paranoid.

The maroon sedan changed lanes, too.

Jessica gripped the steering wheel even tighter. She wasn't being paranoid. That car was following her.

Panic gripped her. Why hadn't she listened to Andrew when he'd warned her not to go out alone?

Suddenly, the maroon sedan sped up and rammed into the back of her car. Jessica was knocked against the steering wheel as the car careened forward. She screamed and grabbed hold of the wheel tighter trying to get the car back under control. A fleeting moment of doubt rushed through her mind. It could have been an innocent accident. But that thought was quickly disregarded when the car revved up and slammed into hers again, propelling her forward. Fear-laced adrenaline pumped through her as horns blared and tires screeched. This maniac was trying to run her off the road. He was trying to kill her!

Jessica glanced in the rearview mirror and saw the car moving beside her. It was going to ram into her again. This time she swerved to miss it, veering into the other lane and nearly slamming into a different car.

She changed lanes again as the maroon sedan swerved

to her side once more and attempted to push her over. Jessica hit the accelerator. Her only chance was to outrun him.

The next exit was coming up. She needed to get off the interstate.

She jerked the wheel, crossing three lanes in one movement. Tires screeched and horns blared again, but Jessica didn't care. She was going to make that exit.

She flew down the off ramp, made a quick right turn and sped through an intersection.

She reached for her phone and hit the speed dial, calling Margo's number. The call went straight to voice mail. Margo must have shut off her phone after talking to Jessica. She hit the speed dial again and called Andrew's number.

He answered on the first ring.

"Andrew, I'm in trouble!"

"What's wrong?"

"Someone's after me. He's ramming my car. He's trying to run me off the road."

"Where are you?"

"Flowood Drive. I was on my way to a call. I'm sorry. I should have listened to you. I shouldn't have gone out alone."

"Hang on. I'm going to call 911 on the other line."

His voice disappeared and Jessica felt his absence from the car. But he was back after a moment.

"Jessica, I have the 911 operator on the line. Tell her where you are."

Jessica called off the location and described the maroon sedan. She spotted the car in the side mirror approaching her again at a high speed. He'd found her. "He's coming after me!" The car rammed hers and Jessica screamed, skidding to keep the car on the road. "He's trying to kill me!"

"I have patrol cars moving to your location," the operator said.

Panic laced Andrew's voice. "Hang on, Jessica. Stay on the line with me. I'm on my way."

The car sped up and tried to get in front of her. Jessica slammed on the brakes and let him skid into the railing before taking off around him.

"Jessica! Are you all right?"

"I'm okay," she said. But the car kept coming. She strained to see the driver's face as he pulled up beside her, but all she saw was the darkness of the car.

He rammed her again, this time causing her to veer off the road. She lost control and the car broke through a fence before skidding to a stop and turning off.

The seat belt locked, throwing her backward against the seat. She fought to catch her breath, uncertain if it was force of the seat belt or pure adrenaline that knocked the air from her.

"Jessica! Are you with me?"

Andrew's voice was a calming balm as she fought to steady her breathing. "I'm here," she managed to say.

"What happened?"

She looked up as the headlights cast a glow on open land. "I went off the road." She tried the ignition but it wouldn't restart. "The car won't crank."

She glanced in the rearview mirror and spotted headlights up on the road. A door slammed and Jessica felt her stomach clench.

"Someone's coming!" What if he was returning to finish the job?

"You should be hearing the sirens approaching you soon," the 911 operator stated. "Do you?"

Jessica strained to hear them over the pounding of her own pulse. The police were on their way…but would they make it in time?

She gripped the steering wheel, torn between her desire to get out and confront this man who was terrorizing her and her common sense commanding her to run. But where could she run to? She was a sitting target, waiting for her predator to attack.

"I want to see who it is," she stated, opening the car door and stepping out.

"Jessica, stay in the car!" Andrew's voice was frantic over the speakerphone.

Part of her was screaming to run, but her stubborn streak wouldn't allow her feet to move. She wanted to see who it was. She wanted to know who was behind this act. What kind of sick person did this to someone?

She sucked in a breath as he drew near. All she could make out in her car's dome light was his outline. It could be anyone.

Robert Young.

The spouse or boyfriend of one of the women at the shelter.

Or some random man she didn't even know about.

"He's coming," she whispered. "He's heading toward me."

"Jessica, get back into the car!"

But as he grew closer, the light from her car began to make his features visible.

She was about to find out.

SIX

Jessica's heart pounded as the man approached. She reached into her purse for the can of mace she kept there. If he was here to start trouble, she was ready for him.

She squinted, trying to make out the features of his face but his ball cap made that impossible.

A flutter of courage welled up inside her. She held out the can, ready to mace him. "That's far enough," she demanded. "Who are you?"

"I just wanted to see if I could offer assistance."

She strained to hear his voice. She didn't recognize it.

"I won't hurt you. My name is Dr. Anthony Upton. I honestly just want to help."

"Take off your hat," Jessica demanded.

He removed his hat and she was able to get a good look. She didn't recognize this man. Was it possible he truly was there to help?

She glanced past him to get a better look at his vehicle. He was driving an SUV, not a sedan.

He must have noticed her relief because he relaxed as well and moved closer. "What happened?"

"Someone was following me. He tried to run me off the road."

The sound of sirens grew louder and a patrol car

stopped at the road. Andrew's car screeched to a halt too, and he jumped out and ran down the embankment.

"Jessica!" He rushed to her and pulled her into his embrace. "Are you okay? Are you hurt?"

"I'm fine. I'm not hurt." But she clung to him, thankful for his presence and his strong embrace as the reality of what she'd been through set in.

As the police arrived, she looked at her car and noticed the dents and torn metal from the multiple hits.

Someone had tried to kill her and, this time, they'd nearly succeeded.

Andrew put his arm around her and led her back toward the road. He wanted to speak with the police, but he wanted to make certain she was safe first.

"I'm sorry, Andrew," she said. "I should have listened to you. I shouldn't have gone out by myself."

He hugged her to him. All he cared about was that she was safe. Hearing her scream, being unable to be there, he'd felt helpless. He didn't want to go through that again.

"I'll be right back." He jogged back down to where the police officers were speaking with the man who'd been standing by the car when Andrew had arrived. The police let him go and Andrew approached them.

"Who was he?"

"Dr. Anthony Bennett. He said he saw your girl run off the road and a maroon sedan speed away. He stopped to help."

"You believe him?"

"He seemed sincere. He also gave us a good description of the car that ran Ms. Taylor off the road. We had several 911 calls describing the same vehicle on the interstate. We're currently conducting a search for that car."

Andrew stared at the mangled mess of Jessica's car.

It was amazing that she'd walked away from it without being seriously injured.

Had God protected her?

He handed over his business card and asked the officer to let him know about any new developments.

He walked back to Jessica and knelt beside her. Her hands shook and she choked back tears.

"You need to go to the hospital."

"I'm fine…physically."

He started to offer to drive her back to the shelter but couldn't bring himself to let her out of his sight. Not just yet. "How about we stop for coffee?"

She nodded her agreement and Andrew got in and drove them to his apartment.

"Where are we?"

"My place. I thought you could use some time to compose yourself before you return to the shelter."

"Thank you. I think that's a good idea."

He walked around and opened her door, then led her up the stairs to his apartment.

She was shivering, but he knew it wasn't from the dropping temperatures. She was frightened. His anger burned at seeing her this way. Robert's tactics would take their toll on even someone as strong as Jessica, whether she wanted to admit it or not.

He kicked up the thermostat a notch just to be sure then went to the kitchen and started the coffee brewing as Jessica moved around his living room. He realized this was the first time she'd ever seen his place.

She glanced at the family photos on his wall then spotted the engagement photo on his desk. She picked it up and studied it. "She's very pretty. Who is she?"

A sudden uncomfortable sensation hit him. It felt odd to talk about Tory to Jessica, yet he realized he wanted to tell her. He wanted her to know all about him. "Her name was Tory. She died two years ago."

"I'm sorry. I know what it's like to lose someone you love."

"Have you lost someone close to you?"

"My brother, Dean. He was killed."

"I'm sorry to hear that."

"Were you and Tory close?"

"Yes. We were engaged actually."

"Andrew, I didn't know you were engaged." She glanced at the photo again. "You looked happy."

"We were."

"How did she die?"

"She was in a boating accident. We'd just had a lot of rain and the Pearl River was high. Tory went out alone. She was always doing that. Running off alone without thinking about her safety. The boat capsized and she drowned."

He grimaced at the memory. He hadn't meant the twinge of bitterness that crept into his voice, but repeating that story reminded him of how reckless Tory had been with her life…and spotlighted how reckless Jessica could be with hers.

He leaned against the counter, recalling the panic that had invaded him earlier knowing Jessica was in danger and there was nothing he could do to help her. She'd found a way to sneak into his life and grant him hope again for a future, but with the life she lived would it be another repeat of his and Tory's relationship? Would he spend his time always wondering and worrying about her?

He wasn't sure he could handle another relationship like that.

Jessica placed the photograph back onto the desk. "I

can see I've upset you. I'm sorry, Andrew. That wasn't my intention."

He turned to look at her. She was so beautiful and he couldn't deny he was captivated by her. But he wanted to know what motivated her to place her life in danger day after day. "I thought we agreed you weren't going to leave the shelter alone. I don't understand, Jessica. What were you thinking?"

She bristled and her defenses went up. "I received a call about a woman in trouble. I had no choice but to go."

"You should have called me."

"I couldn't wait. The sooner I make it to the scene, the better likelihood I can make a difference."

"But you didn't make it to the scene, did you? You walked right into the path of danger and nearly got yourself killed."

"I know you're angry—"

"Angry? No, Jessica, I was petrified." He moved toward her. "I was so afraid I would get there and you would be dead, and I knew there was nothing I could do to stop it." He touched her face, caressing her cheek. "You've become very important to me, and I don't think I could stand to see something happen to you."

His finger stroked her lips and she shivered beneath his touch. All he could think was how much he wanted to kiss her, how much he wanted to feel her lips against his.

Yet uncertainty clouded her eyes and he sensed she wasn't ready for that. Instead, he wrapped her in his embrace and she melted into him, her head fitting perfectly against his shoulder.

He could wait for her to be ready.

Since his plans with Jessica had changed after last night's events, Andrew decided to go into the office.

The Michael Shroud case landed on his desk during the morning meeting. He glanced through the police report. The thirty-six-year-old college professor was accused of domestic assault in the beating of his girlfriend. Neighbors had phoned police when they heard screams from Shroud's apartment. Police arrived to find twenty-two-year-old Amy Vance beaten and bruised. A baseball bat was removed from the household and Shroud arrested. However, Miss Vance refused to acknowledge that Shroud had beaten her.

Andrew closed the file. With no witnesses to the beating and Amy refusing to press charges, it was likely Shroud would not be charged. His prosecutor instincts told him this was a no-brainer. He couldn't win it. But a different instinct told him it wasn't right. There was no doubt what had transpired in that apartment. He looked up Shroud's history and found three more reports of incidents against young female students. No charges were ever filed.

Probably because Shroud terrorized these girls into silence.

His jaw clenched. Six months ago, this case wouldn't even have registered with him, but now…now he saw Sarah in every victim of violence. He wrote down phone numbers of the previous victims. If he could convince them to tell their stories, perhaps he could get a pattern of violent behavior admitted as evidence. It was a long shot. Past behaviors weren't usually admissible, but if he could prove a pattern he might be able to use it against Shroud. That was of course assuming he could convince Amy Vance to press charges. Bill would never let him continue without it.

He smiled thinking about Jessica. He might have a reason to call her in professionally on this matter. He liked the idea of working together with her on this case to get a psycho off the streets.

And maybe he could redeem himself a little in her eyes too.

Jessica reached for a bottle of pain relievers as she readied herself for the day. The chase and subsequent crash last night had left her body sore and her head aching, but that didn't mean she got a day off. She swallowed two pills then picked up the phone and called Margo. Her friend had phoned earlier while Jessica was still asleep and left a voice mail for Jessica to return the call.

But the noise from the bullpen when Margo answered was deafening.

"I can hardly hear you," Jessica told her. "What's going on over there?"

"We're on full alert. An escaped convict was sighted in the area."

"He must be dangerous."

"Very dangerous, according to reports. He was in for murder. I'm trying to track down information about why he would come here, look for family or old girlfriends, that sort of thing. I just got the fingerprint results from the note that was left on your car. There were no fingerprints so whoever left it knew what he was doing. He was obviously wearing gloves."

Jessica sighed. "Which wouldn't have looked suspicious in October to anyone who had seen him." Jessica's mind was whirling. Was Robert really controlled enough to think about such things as wearing gloves? He'd struck her more as the get-in-your-face type of crazy.

"I'm still waiting on the report from the break-in at your house. But I looked into your good Samaritan from last night." Jessica had finally reached Margo last night and filled her in on what had happened and why she'd never made it to the hospital. "He checks out. No record. Pays his bills. Deacon in the church. There's no reason to think he's our guy."

"What about the text pictures?"

"I did a trace on the number. It's one of those pre-paid phones. It'll be difficult to track." Margo's desk phone rang. "I'm sorry, Jess. I wish I had better news to give you. I really have to go."

Jessica hung up, leaving her friend to her work. She had work of her own. She wanted to go by the hospital and try to see Amy Vance since she hadn't made it the night before. The young woman had already had over fourteen hours to rationalize her boyfriend's behavior and convince herself it had somehow been her fault.

Jessica also had another reason to go to the hospital. She wanted to drop in to see how her neighbor was doing and look for any indication that Mrs. Brady's fall hadn't been accidental. She parked in the hospital lot then stopped by the information desk and asked for the room number for Mrs. Brady.

The information clerk typed the name into the computer. "I don't find a record of anyone with that name staying here."

Jessica frowned. Had she misunderstood? Now that she thought about it, Mr. Percy hadn't mentioned which hospital, but Jessica was certain this was the hospital Mrs. Brady regularly used. She supposed her nephew could have taken her to another, a specialty hospital perhaps. She would ask Mr. Percy when she saw him again.

Jessica walked to the elevator. When she rounded the corner, she spotted a familiar face. Andrew was waiting at the elevators. He was in full suit mode and held his briefcase in his hand. But his manner was easygoing as he chatted with a woman in scrubs who was smiling up at him, laughing and flirting.

Jessica felt heat rise in her face. She'd forgotten his charm wasn't especially meant for her. But he had wanted to kiss her last night. She was certain he had. Didn't that mean anything today?

He smiled when he spotted her and left scrubs girl standing there gawking after him. "Hi. What are you doing here?"

She felt a tinge of annoyance at being checked up on, but she pushed that thought away. He wasn't trying to control her. His questions were asked out of concern for her safety. "I borrowed Mia's car and, I know you're worried, but I still need to visit the girl I was going to see last night. She was beaten up by her boyfriend. I was hoping to speak with her, offer her some counseling."

"Amy Vance?"

"How did you know?"

"I'm prosecuting the case. I need to get a statement from her, but the report says she's refusing to press charges or even to acknowledge Shroud hit her."

She couldn't help the disappointment that flowed through her at learning that Andrew had been assigned the case. She knew his history. With no complaining witness, he wouldn't give this case a second look. Amy Vance was just another young girl who would fall through the system because her case wasn't sexy enough to make the local news.

But if that were true then why was he here?

"I want to get this guy, Jessica. Did you know he's attacked three other students in the past two years?" He pulled out his notes and showed her the grim photographs. "I spoke with two of the girls earlier trying to convince them to press charges, but they didn't want to relive it."

Her heart lurched at his words, at the determination and fire she saw in his eyes. She didn't know if it would stick, but she was pleased to see his efforts. Maybe this ordeal with Sarah had reached him.

"Maybe I could talk to them and perhaps convince them to change their minds."

A grin stretched across his face, but it was more than just the smile he flashed to the cameras. This smile was targeted just for her. "I was hoping you would say that. Why don't we go up and see her together?"

Amy Vance was a wisp of a thing, slim and tall with long blond hair that hung around her face. Andrew could tell she was pretty despite the bruises on her face. She wore her arm in a sling with a brace on her left wrist. He knew from the reports that the bones had been shattered. Amy may never have proper use of her hand again.

But she stood firm on her insistence that her boyfriend did not touch her.

"He would never hurt me," she told them both. "He loves me."

Andrew lost patience with her. He pulled out the photos he'd gathered of the other girls her boyfriend had "loved." "Did he love these girls, too?" He tossed one photo after another to her. "He did this to them."

She pushed the photos away. "No, he wouldn't do that."

Jessica sat on the bed and took Amy's good hand. "You don't have to live with this, Amy. We can help you, both of us. I can offer you shelter, a safe place to stay where he can't hurt you. And Andrew—" She turned to look at him. Was that admiration he saw in her face? "Andrew will fight to make sure he pays for what he did to you."

In the end, Amy refused to concede. Her naivety bothered him. Why would she choose to stay with him? That still plagued him. Why would she put up with such abuse?

They left defeated.

Jessica sat on a bench. "She's just not ready."

He couldn't be so nonchalant. "When will she be ready? When he kills her?"

"Amy has classic behaviors of a newly battered woman. She's taking all the blame. You can't force someone to make the choice to leave. They have to come to it on their own. Unfortunately, it will have to get a lot worse before Amy will accept help." She gave a long, weary sigh. "If only I'd made it to the scene things might have been different." She glanced up at him. "Can you make a case without her testimony?"

He sat down beside her. "Doubtful."

"Are you going to try?"

He heard the challenge in her tone and even though it stung he accepted her right to ask it. "I want to get this guy, Jessica."

Her smile lit up her face. Who knew something as simple as a declaration to try could make a person so happy?

"It would really help me if I could get other victims to come forward and state what he did to them."

"I'll contact the college. All of these girls have been students and he's a professor. Surely they have a policy against student/teacher relationships."

He watched the fire igniting in her and smiled. Her passion was amazing. She never gave up, even when her own life was in danger. She saw men like Robert and Michael Shroud and didn't flinch at their threats and violence.

He'd never met anyone like her before.

She caught him staring. "What are you looking at?"

"It's not just a job to you."

"No, it's not. If I can help, if I can offer assistance…" She sighed. "But the truth is most of the time there's not much I can do to help."

"Well, you helped us. Me and Sarah. If it wasn't for you my sister might be dead now. I thank God every day for bringing you into our lives." He stroked her hand, enjoying the way she shivered under his touch.

His phone buzzed at his side, interrupting their private moment. He glanced at the screen and saw a message from his office. "I have to go interview the boyfriend before he's released." He stood to leave then turned back to her, feeling something unfinished and unspoken between them. "I promised Sarah I would come by the shelter tonight. Can I see you, too?" He held his breath, waiting and watching for her response.

A blush filled her face and a slow smile spread across her mouth. "I'll be there."

He sighed, realizing there was no use in denying it anymore. He liked her. "Good. Then I'll see you later tonight."

He hurried from the hospital. He'd promised to see her later, and for the first time in a long time he accepted the fact that he couldn't wait.

SEVEN

Keeping up with Jessica wasn't always easy. Andrew discovered she had a tendency to do as she pleased whenever she pleased. She was used to doing things on her own, but she was trying to keep him aware. He appreciated that. He wasn't looking for total control of her life, but it made him feel better to know she was safe, especially since he didn't want anyone else to suffer because of his sister's poor choices.

Today, she'd agreed to let him accompany her to an appointment at Roman Middle School to do a presentation on domestic violence.

As usual, Jessica was at her best—beautiful and passionate about a cause in which she believed. He was certain she had every eye in the classroom on her…including his.

He'd heard her speak before about domestic violence and violence against women, but today seemed different—she seemed different. Though he realized it was probably only he who had changed. This whole matter with Sarah had been impacting him for months and meeting Jessica, well, he'd certainly evolved since then. She'd pushed him, challenged him to rethink his views and opinions about domestic violence cases. It was because of her that he was becoming a better man.

"Have you ever had a boy who asked you to spy on his ex-girlfriend and report back to him who she was seeing and what she was doing?" Several of the girls nodded, recognizing the behavior. "We call that stalking by proxy. If anyone ever asks you or a friend to do this, you need to tell him no. Not only is he using you, he is also exhibiting controlling and manipulative behavior with the other girl. Oftentimes in cases like these, it doesn't end with just reporting back. He'll often ask you next to do things that make you uncomfortable, like stealing personal items from her or placing notes or reminders from him where she will find them. That's an emotional form of abuse and harassment."

One girl raised her hand and Jessica called on her. "What should we do in that situation?"

"Good question. You should tell someone who can help you, a parent or a teacher. Someone who can put a stop to this type of behavior before it escalates to more serious physical abuse."

"Why should we tell?" another girl commented. "No one will do anything. My mom's boyfriend hit her and she called the cops and two days later this guy was out of jail and back at our house. No one does anything to help."

"Well, that's why I brought my good friend A.D.A. Andrew Jennings along with me today. Andrew, would you come stand up here with me?"

All eyes in the room turned to look at him. Andrew felt put on the spot. That was a dirty trick for Jessica to play on him. He reluctantly stood and walked toward the front of the classroom.

"You see, girls, A.D.A. stands for Assistant District

Attorney. It's Andrew's job to prosecute these fellows that beat up on women. Isn't that right, Andrew?"

"Yes, that's right."

"And how would you, as a representative of the District Attorney's Office, respond to what this young lady just shared?"

Was she baiting him, trying to rope him into a philosophical debate? "We at the District Attorney's office take violence against women very seriously. It's our job to prosecute the offenders to the fullest extent of the law."

"Sounds like a bunch of baloney. What about my mom?" she asked.

He looked at this young girl and realized they'd already lost her to the cycle unless someone—someone like Jessica—intervened and reminded her that she had worth. He pulled a business card from his pocket, knelt before her desk and handed it to her. "Next time that man comes back, you tell your mama to call me."

Andrew helped her carry in her day's purchases. Today, she'd focused on buying necessities for the shelter—washing detergent, toiletries, even new air filters. The common room was empty and Jessica noted the shelter seemed quiet. She didn't worry. According to the schedule posted on the wall, Mia had taken the ladies to a Bible study sponsored by a local church.

They deposited their bags in the kitchen and began unloading. She had to admit she'd expected Andrew accompanying her everywhere would be annoying, but she enjoyed having him along. It felt good to have someone else to depend on for once, someone to help her carry the load she shouldered. And it helped to have a big strong man carry in the heavy items, too.

She ripped the cover off the air filter and grabbed the

stool. The vent was in the hallway and it was better to change it while she was thinking about it.

"Let me do that," Andrew said, but she stopped him. He'd come from work and was wearing a suit and tie. "It's been quite a while since I've changed this air filter. I'd hate for you to get dirt on that suit."

She reached for the vent and the stool wobbled beneath her feet, then tipped over, sending her falling…right into Andrew's waiting arms.

"I've got you," he said, his breath warm against her face.

She stared into his beautiful sea-green eyes. His amused glint darkened and his body tensed. She could feel the strength in his arms on her back and legs as he held her and the line of his shoulders as she clung to him. His gaze roamed her face, zeroing in on her lips. He wanted to kiss her and, despite the way her pulse raced with fear and anticipation, Jessica knew she would let him.

The musky scent of his aftershave overwhelmed her senses. She inhaled but found dust particles mingled in. She sneezed.

"Bless you." Andrew dropped her to her feet, their intimate moment gone.

Had she imagined the desire she'd sensed in him… or in herself?

He picked up the new filter, climbed onto the stool and had it installed in only a moment's time. "There you go. Nothing to it."

Sure, no problem for him and his six-foot-two stature. "Thanks for the help."

He deposited the old filter into the garbage bin then dragged the can toward the kitchen.

She washed her hands in the kitchen sink, noticing

as she did the dust covering his suit. "I'd really like to have that suit cleaned," Jessica said as he swatted at the dust on his jacket.

"It's just a suit. Don't worry about it."

"But I'm sure it cost a pretty penny. I'd feel better if you'd let me."

He draped his jacket over the back of the chair. "I'll tell you what. You give me a slice of that cherry pie and we'll call it even."

She glanced at the pie Deloris had made. She said baking relaxed her, and it made Jessica feel good to have ingredients around for her to indulge.

Jessica took two plates from the cabinet. She left the doors slightly open so he could see the full shelves.

"Looks like you've done some shopping since I was here last."

"Oh, that." She shrugged as if it was no big deal. "We had a very generous donation arrive."

"I'm glad." He cut into his piece. "A place this size probably takes a lot of work, maintenance-wise, I mean. How do you handle everything?"

"I try to do what I can myself. I have volunteers from Margo's church that sometimes come and make minor repairs. They're a real blessing for our little shelter."

"Why do you do it, Jessica? What made you want to open a place like this? A woman like you could be doing anything."

"A woman like me?"

"Smart, strong, attractive. You would probably make a great litigator. You're certainly more fearsome than any defense attorney I've come up against in court."

Jessica felt her face warm. Had he just called her attractive? "I have to be strong. Some of these women don't have anyone else to stand up for them. They're not as fortunate to have family like Sarah is."

He gazed at her. "They have you. I'd say that makes them very fortunate. But I'm curious. What makes a person wake up one day and say 'I think I'll open a shelter for battered women'?"

She hesitated. What would he say if he knew she'd been given this revelation only after becoming one of those battered women? Would he be shocked? Would he still think her fearsome?

She fell back on her standard response. "This is my calling. God made all of this possible. His provision is what keeps us operating, and His strength is what keeps me going."

Andrew stared at her, his eyes curious and suspicious of her answer. She could see he knew there was more to the story and was debating on whether or not to push it. She didn't give him the chance. "What about you? What made you wake up one day and say 'I think I'll be a prosecutor'?"

"I've always hated people that take advantage of others. I think people should know there are consequences to their actions. Unfortunately, what I've seen is that there are always people willing to be taken advantage of. People like Sarah who let any lowlife take control of their lives."

"There's a very complex psychology behind that kind of behavior."

"The thing is, Jessica, it doesn't seem complicated. Someone hits you, someone threatens you, leave. You get out. How hard is that?" He shook his head as he stroked his fork over his plate. "I love my sister, but I don't understand how she let this happen."

Jessica sucked in a breath. He could be talking about

her. He was talking about her. Hot tears burned at the back of her eyes. She batted them back. She wouldn't let him see her cry.

She jumped up and took both their plates to the sink. She didn't understand what was coming over her. She'd dealt with this type of bigotry before. She had educational material on the psychology of battering. But all she could think of, all she could feel, was humiliation that she'd been one of them.

She heard Andrew move behind her and felt his hand on her shoulder. "I'm sorry. I'm just trying to understand all of this."

She took a deep breath, got a grip on her frantic emotions and turned to face him. "If you really want to understand then I'm sure I can find you some material to read." She pushed past him and headed down the hallway toward her office. She heard him following. When she reached her office, she grabbed a handful of pamphlets and held them out to him.

"Some of these are very helpful in understanding the battering behavior."

He reached for her hand instead of the pamphlets. "Jessica, what did I say?" He moved close to her and slipped his other arm around her waist, pulling her to him. His voice became a whisper against her skin. "You're not like these women. You're strong and independent and amazing."

Her head spun as he tightened his arms around her. He was definitely going to kiss her. She longed to get lost in his embrace and feel protected and safe. He was not like other men she'd encountered. He was kind and gentle and he protected those he cared about. She would never have believed such a man really existed.

But he had existed—Dean—and Mitch had killed him.

The man she'd let into their lives had killed her brother. And as Andrew said, she had to live with the consequences of her choice.

"I can't." She pushed him away. She'd vowed never to fall for charisma and a handsome face again, but wasn't that was she was doing? She knew almost nothing about Andrew yet here she was falling into his arms at the first sweet words he uttered.

"What's the matter?"

She stepped into her office shaking her head. "I'm sorry. I just can't." She shut the door and leaned against it as tears streamed down her face.

No matter how her heart craved it, there could never be anything between her and Andrew. He was attracted to a woman who didn't really exist, and she was bound by a trust to her dead brother.

Jessica holed up in her office trying to do paperwork, but her mind kept replaying her encounter with Andrew. She couldn't deny the attraction to him. It had felt so good to be in his arms, but more than that it had felt good to have someone to lean on. Someone to talk with. And it emphasized the emptiness in her life that she'd refused to acknowledge.

The scent of fried chicken drifted into her office. She smiled, knowing Deloris was cooking. It was good to know she was able to have a purpose again. Jessica wished she could as easily give all the others the same sense of purpose.

Jessica put down her work. She wasn't getting anything done anyway, and it was time to get Andrew off her mind. Fellowship with other women was just what she needed.

"I like that boy," Deloris was saying as Jessica entered

the kitchen. "He's good to his sister. That's always a sign of good character."

Jessica noted the group gathered in the kitchen included Mia, Joan, Danielle, Pamela, Deloris and even Margo.

"I thought it was how he treated his mother that showed a sign of good character," Joan said.

"Mother, sister, whomever. The way a man is with the women in his family is how he'll be with the woman he loves."

Jessica poured herself a cup of coffee. "Who are we talking about?"

"Andrew Jennings," Danielle piped up. "We all think you should go for it with him, Jessica. You deserve some happiness in your life."

Jessica choked on her coffee, coughing and struggling to catch her breath. She looked at Danielle. "What? Who said there was anything going on between me and Andrew?"

All heads turned to Mia. "Well, I did catch you two kissing in the hallway this afternoon."

Jessica stared at Mia, stunned by her revelation. "You did not."

"Well, I saw something. If he didn't kiss you, he definitely wanted to."

Sarah entered the kitchen. "Who wanted to do what?"

Danielle piped up again. "Your brother. He likes Jessica. And Jessica likes him back. What do you think, Sarah? Don't you think they'd make a cute couple?"

Sarah looked at Jessica then shrugged. "I think a relationship would be good for him. Maybe then he'd butt out of my life."

Jessica was surprised to hear the bitterness in Sarah's voice. "What do you mean? He's looking out for you."

"He's always thought he knew what was best for me. I'm tired of him second-guessing my decisions."

"Well, honey, since you're here, I'd say your decisions needed second-guessing," Deloris told her.

Sarah looked stunned by her words, then angry. "Why can't you all just leave me alone?" She stormed from the kitchen.

Jessica started to go after her.

"Let her go," Deloris advised. "She's just feeling a little confined, I think. Her whole world has been turned upside down. I know the feeling. Give her some time and she'll get her head together."

"I don't know," Margo said. "The last time I heard you talk like that, Deloris, you went back to Ray."

Jessica shook her head. "How can she say such things about Andrew? He's been nothing but good to her."

"He does call her a lot," said Pamela, a recovering addict who'd been stalked and raped by her boyfriend. "And she always goes off by herself when he does, like she doesn't want anyone to hear. I understand wanting privacy and all, but why such secrecy with her brother?"

Joan nodded. "I've noticed that, too. And she's getting more and more irritable by the day. Maybe her brother isn't the nice guy we all think he is."

Danielle nodded her agreement. "It wouldn't be the first time we've been fooled by a handsome, charming man. I don't think a one of us can claim to have great judgment in that area."

Several of them nodded and looked as if they were processing that. Jessica was surprised by their lack of trust. "Andrew isn't like that. I would know." She noticed the looks that passed between them. They thought she was being blinded by her attraction to him.

She looked at Margo, knowing she could always count on her for an honest opinion. "What do you think?"

"Well, there's no record of any assault or domestic violence calls to his residence."

"You ran his background?"

Margo shrugged. "Of course. I do background checks on most men I meet. I know, I know, it's obsessive. I'm working on getting better."

"So you think he's okay?"

"He's a public figure, so I think I would have heard if there were anything fishy about him, but it's hard for me not to be wary of a man who's getting close to someone I care about. Just don't fall too hard for him until you're sure you know him."

Jessica glanced around the room. All of these women, including Margo, were so wounded. How could they possibly make sound decisions about a man's character? But wasn't she one of them? How could she trust her own judgment? She thought Andrew was a good guy, but then she'd been wrong about Mitch. Was it possible Andrew was not what he seemed? And what about these mysterious, secret phone calls?

She had to at least consider the possibility.

He gathered up files and headed home. He would have a lot of reading to do tonight, but that suited him fine. Andrew wanted to get as much background information as he could on Professor Shroud, whether or not Jessica could convince Amy Vance to press charges against him.

He stopped by the deli and picked up a roast beef plate for supper. Too bad Jessica wasn't coming over to help him. He liked the way they meshed on this case. Why had he ever been so annoyed by her?

He checked his mail then climbed the stairs to his

apartment, dropping the food on the counter and the case files onto the couch. He was already halfway through his roast beef and carrots when he took a break. After scanning through the mail, he tossed the junk into the trash. He opened his cell phone bill and skimmed through it, noting the calls made to and from Sarah's phone.

He'd always paid her bill to make certain she had a means to call for help when she needed it. Two outgoing calls had been made to one number—one number he recognized. Several incoming calls had been received from that same number as recently as the day the bill was printed, three days prior. The calls ranged from ten to thirty minutes in length.

His gut clenched and he pushed away his food, losing his appetite.

Sarah was talking to Robert.

Jessica hung up the phone in her office exasperated and concerned. She'd phoned every hospital in the metro area and none listed Mrs. Brady as a patient. Of course, with HIPAA confidentiality she knew she might not be able to get information on her condition, but most hospitals gave you room numbers of admitted patients.

She tried Mr. Percy's number instead. No answer. She tried several more times as she went about her morning, but by lunch, she'd grown worried. It wasn't like him not to answer. What if something had happened to him? What if he'd fallen like Mrs. Brady? He didn't have any family to come in and help him out.

She wanted to go over there and make certain he was okay. Perhaps she could locate Mrs. Brady's nephew and find out which hospital he'd taken her to. For all she knew, her injury could have required admittance to a nursing facility or he could have brought her home by now to care for her there.

A wave of fear swept through her at the idea of going there alone. The memory of realizing Robert had been inside her house—and possibly run her off the road—stopped her. What if he was out there waiting for her to go off alone again?

You can't stop true love.

She shuddered and reached for the phone once more. With only a few exceptions, she hadn't left the shelter without Margo or Andrew going with her. She hated to bother Margo while she was on the job. With this new threat of an escaped convict in town, Margo was getting the opportunity to work with the FBI in tracking this escaped convict. While Jessica hoped the man didn't harm anyone, she was glad for the bump it was giving Margo's career.

She dialed Andrew's number, annoyed when it went directly to voice mail. He only turned it off when he was in court, and she remembered him saying he had several arraignments to handle today.

She glanced at the time. He could be tied up in court for hours, and Jessica felt an urgency to make certain Mrs. Brady was safe. She should wait for him. She knew she should…but what if Mrs. Brady needed her?

She sighed, frustrated with his and Margo's constant need to keep tabs on her. She only wanted to check on her neighbor. What harm could come from that? She grabbed her purse and went to find Mia.

"May I borrow your car again?"

Mia gave her a skeptical look but handed over the keys. "Where are you going?"

"I'm going home to check on my neighbors. I have a bad feeling. I'll be back soon."

Mia looked as if she wanted to stop her, but Jessica didn't give her the opportunity. She marched out to the car and got in. She was tired of being treated like a victim. She wasn't going to allow Robert to dictate her life any longer.

Jessica drove to her neighborhood and pulled into her own driveway. She walked across the street to Mr. Percy's and knocked on the door. Several days of newspapers were piled up on the driveway indicating he hadn't been out to get them. Had he fallen? Was he lying alone inside unable to get help?

She peeked through a window but couldn't see him. She called his name and pounded on the door then listened for the sound of someone crying out. She heard nothing and the house was locked up tight.

She hated how her mind always went to the worst. But he'd taken Marlon. Shouldn't she at least hear the little dog barking inside? Perhaps he was visiting Mrs. Brady. She stared at the house across the way. For several days? If he wasn't there, she was calling 911 and having someone sent to check on him.

She walked across the street and headed up to Mrs. Brady's house. The garage door was open, revealing her car still sitting in its parking space, but no other car was visible. What was this nephew of hers driving?

She knocked on the door and called out. No noise came from inside. She walked around to the back to check the sliding doors that led into the kitchen and gasped at what she saw. Mrs. Brady's kitchen was always cluttered with baking pans and cooking utensils, but now it looked as if someone had been squatting there. Beer cans were stacked on the table and fast food bags and wrappers were scattered on the floor. She tried the door, finding it unlocked, and pushed it open. She was immediately assaulted by the stench of cigarette smoke. Mrs. Brady didn't smoke.

Anger burned inside her as she realized Mrs. Brady's nephew was trashing her home. What kind of way was that to take care of his aunt? She only hoped she wouldn't find Mrs. Brady laid up in a filthy bed without being cared for. Her heart broke at the idea of what she might find. She needed to be in a hospital or a facility that could help her recuperate, not trapped inside her home while some distant nephew took her for everything she had.

Jessica walked back toward the bedrooms, calling her name. Movement at the corner of her eye startled her and she spun around but saw no one. "Hello?" she called. "It's Jessica Taylor from next door. I didn't mean to frighten anyone, but I wanted to check on Mrs. Brady."

No response.

She glanced toward where she'd seen the movement, scanning the den for any proof of someone there. She knew she'd seen something, but no one was visible now.

She headed toward Mrs. Brady's bedroom again, slowly pushed open the door and was assaulted by an overpowering stench. "Mrs. Brady. It's Jessica from next door checking on you." A figure lay unmoving on the king-size bed, covered head to toe with a blanket. "Mrs. Brady?" Fear ripped through Jessica. No one should be that still.

She reached for the blanket and pulled back the cover, stifling a scream that bubbled up inside her. It was Mrs. Brady, dead, her throat slashed and the stench of death surrounding her.

Her cell phone buzzed and she glanced at it. A text message appeared.

I'm coming for you next.

* * *

Jessica sat on her own porch steps and watched the activity taking place next door. The cops had arrived and encircled the house. Jessica trembled, remembering the frightened look frozen on Mrs. Brady's face. She'd been so scared.

She heard a noise beneath her and glanced down to find Marlon once again taking refuge beneath her porch. How had he gotten free again? The dog shied away from her at first, but after she called to him he finally came. She scooped him up in her arms and petted him. What was he doing here? He was supposed to be with Mr. Percy...wherever he was. She glanced at the house next door. Mrs. Brady had been murdered. Had something happened to Mr. Percy, as well? Was Marlon hiding because he'd seen one or both of them killed? She checked him out, relieved to find him unharmed.

Andrew's car screeched to a stop in front of her house and he jumped out and ran toward her. "I just heard. Are you okay?" He slipped his arm around her and she allowed it, welcomed it. She didn't want to be alone right now.

"I found her. She was murdered. She looked so scared."

"What have the police said? Is Margo over there?"

As if on cue, Margo appeared walking slowly toward them. Her expression indicated what she had to say wasn't good. But then what good news could she bring? Mrs. Brady was dead and there was no changing that.

Andrew stood to face her. "What did you find?"

"She was definitely murdered. We found what we think was the knife that slit her throat. The guy had the nerve to run it through the dishwasher and put it back into the set."

"Do you know who did this? Was it the nephew?"

"We've canvassed the rest of the neighborhood. No one else has even heard that she had a nephew."

"Mr. Percy said he'd met him. He described him to me—tall, dark hair. He said he reminded him of one of those slick used-car salesmen."

"Well, Mr. Percy is MIA. I had a couple of uniforms break into his home and he's definitely not there. One of the neighbors said she hadn't seen him out and about in several days and she was getting worried. She was just about to call someone. We'll check out the hospitals and see if he turns up. Right now, he's our best shot at finding out what happened here."

"You don't think he's…"

Margo sat down on the step beside her. "I don't know what to think right now. Don't worry. We'll find him." She took a deep breath then sighed. "There's something else. We found a lot of surveillance equipment in the kitchen. Cameras and binoculars. Jessica, they were right in the window that overlooks your house."

Andrew shook his head in disbelief. "I knew Robert was dangerous, but I never thought he would be capable of this. Murdering an old woman?"

"No," Jessica said. "Something hasn't felt right to me about all of this. This isn't Robert's style. This may be someone else."

"Someone else stalking you? Any idea who it could be?"

"No. I just don't think… I don't believe this fits Robert's style. From what I've learned from Sarah and the police reports, he's much more physically aggressive."

Andrew grimaced. "What's more aggressive than killing someone? Besides, I've learned never to underestimate what someone is capable of. This was Robert. I feel it in my gut."

Margo nodded her agreement. "Still, I'll go back through our old files and see if there are any new players just released from prison that might want to torment you. Does any particular name come to mind?"

Mitch. This was definitely his style. But he was locked up two states away. She shrugged. "These guys all seem to play by the same book. *Top Ten Ways to Terrorize your Girl.*" She laughed even though it wasn't funny then looked at Margo. "Adam Carey. He loved to play these mind games with Deb."

"You think he's doing this to get you to tell him where his wife is?"

"This guy could have killed me on several occasions when these pictures were snapped. He wants me to know he's in control, that he can get to me whenever he wants. He probably is enjoying watching me squirm and so he keeps raising the stakes. He could also be trying to break me down so that when he finally does confront me, I'm too emotionally shattered to fight back."

Margo nodded. "I'll make a call to my buddy in the Jacksonville P.D. and ask him to drive by the safe house to make sure Deb is okay. We may need to move her to another location. I know you would never tell him where she is, but—"

"Better safe than sorry. And Margo, don't tell me where you send her. I don't want to be responsible for him getting to her."

She nodded then returned to the crime scene next door.

Andrew stared at Jessica. "You do realize if it is him then he will probably kill you if you don't tell him where his wife is."

Chills rushed through her at the thought. Despite what Andrew must think, she didn't want to become a target, but she couldn't betray the trust anyone had placed in her. She clutched Marlon to her. "And if I do tell him, he will definitely kill her. I won't let that happen."

EIGHT

"We're ready to start," Mia said, interrupting the conversation Jessica and Margo were having in the hallway about what to do with Marlon. Margo had suggested the animal shelter, but Jessica was thinking about keeping him as a mascot for Dean's Den.

"Thank you, Mia. Will you put Marlon back into his kennel in my office?" She held out the little dog but Mia backed away, her eyes wide and terrified.

"Do I really have to?"

"He's just a little dog."

In response, Marlon growled as Mia's hands came near him, and his high-pitched yap made her turn and rush away.

Margo flashed her a look. "That girl is weird."

"A lot of people are afraid of dogs. I'll go put him up."

She put Marlon into his carrier then locked it so he couldn't escape. She arrived back in the common room as the women were finding their seats. Three times a week, a counselor came to lead a support group. Margo hardly ever missed a meeting.

She scanned the group. "Where's Sarah?"

"She's not ready." Sarah had refused to join the group today, but Jessica was confident she would change her mind. Because domestic violence often occurred in the privacy of the home, few women had someone in their lives who understood what they were going through. Though with a group, Sarah would have a roomful of women who understood.

Margo turned her gaze toward Jessica and studied her. "What about you? Are you ready yet?"

Every now and then Margo asked her that question. Jessica's reply was always the same. "No."

Margo found a chair in the circle. Jessica stayed back by the door. It wasn't fair to expect the others to open up about their painful ordeals when she never had, but her experiences with Mitch were buried so far inside her she was certain dredging them up again would be too emotional. Besides, Jessica could support these women much better with a clear head and detached emotions.

When it came time to share, Margo was the first to volunteer. "He was standing by the foot of my bed when I awoke." Her voice trembled as she recalled the details of the night that had changed her life and sent her on the path toward police work and a desire to help the weak and wounded. "I couldn't see his face because of the darkness. He was only a shadowy outline. At first, I didn't think he was real. But when he grabbed me, I knew. He clamped his sweaty hand over my nose and mouth. I couldn't scream. I couldn't even breathe. He raped me in my own bed, in my own apartment. Then he was gone.

"He took everything from me. My sense of self, my peace of mind. I had a fiancé who couldn't even touch me anymore without me reliving that night. I wasn't safe in my own home. I had to move. My life was a mess. I had nowhere to turn."

As Margo continued her story, several women hung their heads and sobbed. Jessica knew they could relate.

They'd shared similar experiences although not with strangers.

"I was so ashamed. I joined the force believing if I was strong enough, no one would ever dare mess with me again. But I know now I wasn't as strong as I believed. I wanted people to think I was tough, but the truth was that I was weak and afraid of losing control. Then an amazing thing happened…I lost control. I hit rock bottom, and with nowhere else to fall, I fell to my knees and asked God for help.

"Slowly but surely, He lifted me up. He poured out His love for me, and I soaked it up. I discovered I didn't have the first clue about what it meant to be a strong woman. I didn't understand it until I found the Lord."

She turned and glanced back at Jessica, and Jessica felt a jolt. She'd listened to Margo's story on several occasions, but today was different. Today, Margo seemed to be speaking directly to her, about her and her situation. Why was it she had never put those together before?

A tear slipped from her eye and she brushed it hastily away. No one could ever call Margo weak or burdened. She'd been victimized, but she certainly wasn't a victim any longer. She'd overcome her trauma to the point where she could openly share about the ordeal while Jessica still couldn't even tell her best friend what had happened. How did that make her strong?

She got up and left the room, leaning on the wall outside as more tears threatened to spill over. Voices from inside the room flowed out to her as other women began to speak up about their own experiences. Jessica longed to be inside that room, sitting in the circle and sharing with the group. Suddenly, all she wanted was to go back in time to when Margo asked her that question—was she ready to share?

She was ready.

But instead of stepping toward the door, she walked away from it. A thousand reasons why she shouldn't suddenly flooded her. She had a position to uphold. She'd founded this shelter and this ministry. She couldn't go backward, back to the time when she was the one who needed help. She was the one who was supposed to do the helping. Wasn't that what God had called her to do?

She knew it was a reflex stemming from fear and uncertainty, but she couldn't push through the maze of it all. Next time she would listen to her gut. Next time when Margo asked her that question she would quickly speak up. Next time she would be brave.

She hurried down the hall toward her office before the burning tears that pushed at her eyes finally broke through. She closed the door and let them flow.

Next time.

"The president of Westbrook College claims you're stirring up trouble with one of his professors," Bill said as he motioned Andrew into his office.

"I'm investigating the possibility that Shroud has assaulted other students."

"And what have you found?"

"Three different police reports from the city police. They were called in by the hospital after each girl came into the ER with serious injuries. I want to subpoena the campus security reports for each one and possibly even their records to confirm they were in his classes."

"Are any of these girls willing to testify against him?"

"No. The victims all refused to press charges. I've tried contacting each of them and they're still not ready."

"What about this girl he's accused of assaulting this time?"

"She's also refusing to press charges, but I believe if we continue—"

"We have no complaining witness therefore we have no case. Stop investigating and move on, Andrew." He downed a handful of antacids, a clear indicator to Andrew that he wasn't in the mood for discussion.

But Andrew couldn't let this go so easily. "We have to stop this guy before he kills someone."

"I know you've been going through some stuff with your sister, so I've been turning a blind eye—"

"This isn't about Sarah."

"But you have other, more important cases on your desk to handle, cases where the victims want justice. You can't let this thing with your sister color your judgment. There's no case here. It's time to let this one go."

"Bill—"

"You have my decision, Andrew. Move on to your other cases."

Andrew walked out. A year ago, he wouldn't have blinked at Bill's demand. He stormed into his office and closed the door. He ran his hands through his hair as he admitted the truth.

A year ago, he wouldn't have given Amy Vance a second look.

Jessica sat in her office trying to concentrate on work, but the thump of rain against her window matched her mood—dreary and glum. A day of soul-searching had that effect on her, especially when she realized how lonely her life had become.

She'd shut down after Dean's death, walking the fine line between helping and getting involved. No one knew her, not really. Not even Margo. It was a lonely existence and one she was ready to shed.

A knock at her door caused her to jump, but when she looked up and saw Andrew, rain glistening on his hair and his overcoat damp, the warmth of his smile eased her melancholy mood.

"Looks like you're doing some pretty serious thinking. Were you thinking about me?"

She stared at him dumbfounded by his suggestion. How had he known where her thoughts had been heading? But when she noticed the silly grin on his face, she realized he was only teasing. Heat rose to her face as his eyes widened with pleasurable surprise.

"You were thinking about me." But then the lilt in his voice was replaced with a much more serious tone as he stepped into her office and closed the door. "I'm glad, especially after how we left it here the other day. I owe you an apology for trying to kiss you. I misunderstood. I thought I felt something—"

"You did. We both did." She got up and walked around the desk.

He took her hand in his and closed the distance between them. "Then what happened? I really like you, Jessica. I'm sorry if I pushed too hard."

"You're the first man I've trusted enough to get that close to in a very long time. That's how much I like you."

"But it's not enough, is it? You shrank away from me when I touched you. Will you ever really trust me?"

"I want to. I really do." And she meant it. She'd never wanted anything as much as she wanted to find comfort in his arms. Yet she flinched when he reached out to caress her cheek.

"I will never hurt you, Jessica. I know the kind of men you see every day, but I'm not like them. I promise."

Oh, how she wanted to believe that. Her every instinct was to lose herself in his embrace. His very presence was invigorating—the span of his shoulders, the warmth of his smile, even the scent of the rain on his hair. She leaned into his hands, soaking in the feel of him. His hands on her face sent a thrill through her nerve endings, and she quivered with the anticipation of his lips as they touched hers and sent a rush of emotions through her, both pleasant and painful. He'd shattered the wall she'd so craftily built and all that emotion poured from her in one giant gush.

Sobs tore from her. Tears spilled from her eyes. She didn't want him to see her this way, so out of control, so vulnerable. She tried to pull away but Andrew grasped her hands and held them.

"Don't push me away, Jessica."

He had no idea how much she wanted to believe in him. How much she wanted to trust him. She was so tired of being alone, and he seemed like such a good man. But could she ever really trust her own judgment again?

"I'm a mess." She wiped at the tears streaming down her face.

He held her face in his so she couldn't turn away. "You're a beautiful mess," he said as he kissed her tears away.

Soon, she couldn't distinguish tears of sadness from the tears of joy.

Andrew whistled as he walked back to his car. He'd been whistling a lot lately, but then Jessica seemed to have that effect on him.

He hadn't told her any of the things he'd come to say… how Bill had closed the Shroud case, about Sarah's phone calls to Robert, none of the important business matters he'd wanted to discuss with her.

He smiled. They'd had more important business matters to discuss, and he was pleased with the outcome of their conversation.

Still, she needed to know about Sarah talking to Robert. He turned back to go inside and tell her. Movement from the side of the building caught his attention. He stopped and looked again, noticing a couple locked in an embrace beneath the patio covering, obviously trying to hide.

He couldn't make out faces in the light of dusk but he knew it must be someone from the shelter. Who else would be hiding out back? His heart sank at the thought of telling Jessica one of her residents was making up with her abuser. He remembered the way she'd reacted to Amy's snub. This would be heartbreaking for her.

Andrew got out of his car and headed toward them. "What's going on back here?"

The man turned and swore, but it was the sound of the girl's voice that stopped Andrew cold.

"Don't hurt him."

Sarah!

Andrew's stomach churned. It wasn't... It couldn't be...

He recognized the man's gait as he turned and approached. His face came into clear view and Andrew saw the smug, twisted grin he wore. "I told you that you couldn't keep her from me, Andrew. We belong together."

Anger ripped through him as every muscle clenched. Rain pelted his face but he didn't care. This man had terrorized Sarah and Jessica and may have even killed a little old lady. He had to get Sarah away from him. He stepped toward Robert. His tone held a threat, one he was certain his brother-in-law would understand. "Stay away from my sister."

"No, you stay away or you might just have a little

accident…if you know what I mean." Robert flashed him the same smug smile he'd seen at the office.

Andrew's fists itched to make a statement of their own. "You can't intimidate me the way you do Sarah. I'm not afraid of you."

Robert smiled a threatening, sinister smile that sent chills through Andrew. "You should be. You and your girlfriend in there. Sarah is mine, Andrew. All mine." He grinned again and turned toward Sarah. "Isn't that right, baby?"

Tears streamed down her face intermixing with the rain as she stared at Andrew, but the guilty expression stabbed at him. "I'm sorry, Andrew. I love him."

"Sarah, he's a killer. He murdered Jessica's neighbor."

"More lies," Robert insisted. He turned to Sarah. "Don't you see how they're trying to turn you against me?"

Sarah turned back to Andrew. "You don't know him like I do. He is not a killer." Her eyes pleaded with him to understand.

He tried a different tactic. "Come with me and we'll talk about it."

Hope flashed on her face, but Robert grabbed her arm. "She's leaving with me." He jerked her to him. "Isn't that right, Sarah?"

"Get your hands off her!" Andrew demanded.

Robert's hand came out of nowhere and shoved him away from Sarah. He fell backward and hit the ground.

"Please don't hurt him," Sarah yelled, a comment which infuriated Robert.

"Whose side are you on?" he demanded, backhanding her so hard she fell to the pavement.

Andrew leaped to his feet. "Don't you touch her again!" He tried to push past Robert to reach her, but

Robert's fist came out of nowhere and pain ripped through his jaw.

Robert stood over him. "Now you're going to pay, Andrew, you and that girlfriend you brought into my house. You're both going to pay for what you did to me."

Jessica rushed from her office as the alarm sounded.

Mia came running toward her. "There are two men fighting out back."

Jessica ran to the door and spotted the struggle taking place in the parking lot. "Call 911 and lock this door behind me."

She heard a woman scream. "And do a head count." She ran to the side of the building to find Sarah there crying and screaming. She grabbed Jessica's arm. "Make them stop!"

Glancing at the two men, she realized Andrew was one of them. She had a pretty good idea who the other man was. Fear pulsed through her. Robert had made all their lives miserable and may have killed someone she cared about deeply. What would he do now to Andrew? She couldn't let this fight escalate.

She rushed toward them. "Stop it! Both of you! The police are on their way."

She grabbed hold of Andrew's arm and tried to pull him away. He turned to her, taking his eyes off Robert for only a second before Robert punched him, knocking Andrew to the ground.

Jessica stepped between them, her determination to protect those she cared about overriding the terror she felt at facing this man. "I said stop!" She stared down Robert. "You need to leave. Now!"

He wiped his mouth then spit blood at her feet. Jessica refused to cower in front of this man. She would not allow him to continue to intimidate her with his threats. She wouldn't let him win.

Finally, he nodded toward Sarah. "Let's go, babe."

Andrew scrambled to his feet. "She's not going anywhere with you."

Jessica stopped him before he rekindled the brawl.

Robert turned and walked away. After a moment, Sarah followed behind him.

Andrew looked mortified. "Sarah?"

She turned back and gave him a pitiful look that quickly turned to indignation. "This is my life, Andrew, and I'm tired of you telling me what to do." She spun on her heel and rushed toward Robert's car parked down the street.

They roared past together moments later.

Andrew stared after the car, a look of despair and defeat falling over him. "I can't believe she left with him." He looked at Jessica. "She left with him."

She put her arms around him. There was little she could say that would comfort him now.

Andrew leaned into the sink in the small bathroom off Jessica's office. He cupped water into his hand then rubbed it over his face. He could wash away the blood, but he could never wash away Sarah's betrayal.

He stared at himself in the mirror. How had he let this happen? An hour ago, everything in his life seemed to make sense. Now, nothing did.

Why had this happened? Why had Sarah chosen to go with Robert again? He'd tried so hard to help her. Was there something he could have done differently?

He wanted to fall to his knees and cry out to God, but the only question that came to him was why.

Why, God?

The office door opened and Jessica entered carrying a tray. He saw her look for him on the couch then glance around when he wasn't there, spotting him through the cracked bathroom door.

She set down the tray. "I brought you an ice pack and some pain relievers. I thought you might need them."

He hadn't lost it all. He had Jessica.

She went straight into his arms without hesitation. That meant the world to him, but it also mattered that she didn't lie and tell him everything would be okay. She knew the danger Sarah had chosen just as he knew. But it was her presence that was his comfort.

"I'm sorry," he told her. "When I saw him with her..."

She shushed him. "You don't have to explain to me."

"This is my fault. I saw him trying to coax Sarah into leaving with him, and I knew I had to stop him. Instead, I made the decision easier for her."

"She made her own choice, Andrew."

A knock on the door drew both their attentions. Mia peeked her head in. "I'm sorry to disturb you, but the police are here."

Margo pushed open the door and stepped around Mia. Her surprised expression reminded Jessica of how they must look, her wrapped in Andrew's arms. She pulled away.

"Margo, why are you here?"

"I heard the 911 on the police scanner. I have to admit this wasn't quite what I expected to find when I arrived."

"This isn't what it looks like. Sarah left with her husband."

"I know. I saw her. They stopped one of the patrol cars responding to the 911 call. Robert is going to swear out a complaint against Andrew for assault. I'm sorry, but I have to take him into custody."

* * *

And suddenly his day had gotten even worse.

Andrew remained quiet as he went through the booking process. He was waiting in the holding cell when Bill appeared at the gate.

He didn't look happy, but Andrew didn't expect him to. An A.D.A. mixed up with fighting. It looked bad on the office, and Bill was preparing for a tough election campaign in a few months.

He motioned for the guard to open the cell and Andrew stepped out. He handed him his valuables that had been taken and tagged. Andrew dug through the envelope. He put back on his watch and pushed his wallet into his pocket.

The lecture he expected came as they stepped outside.

"There won't be a prosecution."

"Yes, there will. I didn't start that fight. He did. I'm filing charges against him."

"No, you're not, Andrew. You're going to apologize to him."

"Absolutely not."

"Andrew, you punched the man. Your sister is his witness. And this isn't the first time."

"I was defending my sister, both times."

"The news channels are going to pick up on this story unless you make it go away. This is bad press for our office, Andrew. Do you want all your cases tainted by an assault conviction? Do you want to lose everything you've worked for all these years?"

"None of that is more important than my sister's safety." He faced down his boss. He knew what this was really about—politics.

Bill gave him a stern look. "I've given you a lot of leeway with this matter concerning your sister, Andrew, but I won't have this office dragged through the mud because you have a vendetta against your brother-in-law. Apologize, don't apologize—I don't care. Just clean up this mess."

"Thank you for coming with me," Jessica told Mia as she pulled into her driveway. "Andrew and Margo insist I have someone with me wherever I go. And besides—" she glanced over at her neighbor's home "—I didn't feel comfortable coming here alone."

"I don't mind," Mia said, unloading boxes from the backseat of the car. "So you're really going to give up your place and move into the shelter permanently? Isn't that pretty extreme?"

"I can't stay here, not after what happened to Mrs. Brady because of me."

She unlocked the front door and walked inside. Her life had been turned upside down over the past ten days. She felt like a different person stepping into her house. And her living room seemed a memory, evidence enough for her that it was time to give up this sanctuary and move permanently into the shelter. It was the logical decision and she couldn't say now why she'd resisted for so long.

She dropped her keys onto the coffee table and set down her bag. Most of her belongings were impersonal enough that she felt safe putting them in storage for a while. She could hire someone to do that. But there were several items she wanted with her—her photographs of Dean, the photo album that contained pictures of their childhood, her grandmother's Bible and the silver cross necklace Dean had bought her for their last Christmas together. She stuffed the stack of mail into her bag then went to the bedroom to pack a suitcase.

She was nearly packed when her chimes sounded. Her

heart stopped. Someone was on the porch. The chimes halted abruptly. Jessica picked up her phone and walked into the living room.

Mia, who was packing books, looked to her. "Someone is out there."

Jessica stepped to the window and peeked through the peephole just as someone knocked on the door.

Sarah was standing on her porch.

How did Sarah even know where she lived?

Her heart fluttered. Perhaps she'd had a change of heart already.

She unlocked the door and opened it only to be met with the force of someone pushing their way inside. Sarah was not alone. Robert shoved on the door and Jessica was unable to hold him back. The force sent her reeling backward. She landed hard on her back, the breath knocked from her.

Mia screamed and ran toward the rear of the house. The back door slammed a moment later, indicating she had gotten away.

Robert didn't bother chasing after Mia. He hovered over her, the gun tucked into his pants clearly visible.

"I warned you not to mess with me." He grabbed her arms and pulled her up, his sneer now fully visible. "You and Andrew have been making a mess out of my life. It's time to return the favor." He smacked her across the face, sending her reeling again. Her jaw bucked the arm of the chair as she landed against it.

"Stop it, Robert. Don't hurt her." Sarah's voice behind her was sincere and concerned.

"Don't tell me what to do." He backhanded Sarah.

Jessica saw her glance her way and for the first time noticed the fresh new injuries on her face and neck and her tear-stained cheeks. She'd only been with this man a few hours and already he was back to beating her. He was on a violence roll which meant they were both in real danger.

He grabbed Jessica's purse and tossed it to Sarah. "Grab the money and cell phone."

Sarah dug through the purse as Robert tore through the living room obviously looking for valuables.

Jessica dared a glance at Sarah again. "Are you all right?" she asked.

Sarah nodded but made no move to help her. She pulled out the measly forty dollars Jessica had in her wallet. "This is all she has."

Robert took the cash then grabbed Jessica by the hair. "Where's your money?"

"I don't have any money. That's all I have. I promise."

"Don't lie to me," he warned her. "I know people are all the time giving money to these causes. You must have a stash somewhere."

"No. All the donations go into a fund. I don't have—"

He slammed his hand into her midsentence and Jessica fell against the wall as pain ripped through her face.

Sarah screamed but Robert was not finished with her yet. He yanked her to her feet and smacked her again before pulling her toward him. "Did you really think you could stick your nose into my business and I wouldn't cut it off?"

Fear choked her. He was going to kill her and Sarah was going to watch. *Lord, I don't want to die!* She tossed a pleading look to Sarah, noting the young woman didn't seem to know what to do.

"Robert, don't do this. She was nice. She helped me."

He smacked her across the cheek. "She kept you from me. That can't go unpunished."

This wasn't it. This wasn't how she wanted to die.

Not at the hands of a slime like Robert Young. And what about Andrew? She'd finally found a good man to love. She'd finally been given a second chance. And after losing Tory, could he stand to lose someone else he cared about?

A peace settled over her and suddenly all the training Margo had taught her pushed past the fear. When Robert turned back to her, she used her palm to smack him at the bridge of his nose. He swore and screamed but released her, and Jessica took off running. Not fast enough. He grabbed her before she reached the door and pulled her back. She wriggled on the floor trying to free herself of him, but he overpowered her and was quickly on top of her, pinning her to the floor with his knees.

He barked an order to Sarah. "Get me something to tie her up with."

Sarah backed away, unwilling to comply, but Jessica was uncertain for how long Sarah's hesitancy would last. She kicked and struggled trying to free herself from this man's grasp, but his overpowering weight was no match for her.

He swore again at Sarah then got up and dragged Jessica kicking and screaming across the room. As he reached for the TV cord, she managed one good kick that hit its mark at his knee. It buckled and he fell, but he quickly recovered and hit her, sending her reeling. She fell against the coffee table, hitting her head and shattering the wood beneath her. The room began to spin at the impact of her fall. She felt sick and knew she would be soon if she lived long enough. The room spun in and out of focus. She saw Robert yank the cord from the wall. He grabbed her hands and tied them. She was helpless to move to escape. She was going to die...and she would never have the chance to tell Andrew how much she loved him.

"What do you want with me?" she managed to ask weakly as the room began to dim.

He hovered over her, his face inches away. "I want my revenge."

She saw something above his head, a flash of wood that came crashing down over him. Robert collapsed, landing on top of her. Sarah's screams seemed so far away. Jessica tried to move, willing all her remaining strength to lift her head to see who had come to her rescue.

"What are you going to do with him?" a voice asked. It sounded like a woman's voice, familiar but garbled by the pounding in her head. Sarah? Mia? Had she found someone to help that quickly?

"I have a plan," a man's voice responded.

She tried to focus on the voices and finally latched on to a figure standing over Robert, who lay unmoving on the floor. Jessica saw a pair of jean-clad legs, and when her rescuer moved toward her, she thought she saw cowboy boots.

Clomp, clomp.

Clomp, clomp.

And when he was close enough, he knelt beside her and grinned, that sadistic, smug grin that haunted her nightmares.

Mitch!

"I think it's time we eliminate the boyfriend."

Andrew! He was talking about eliminating Andrew! She tried to scream but darkness finally enveloped her.

NINE

Andrew dialed Jessica's cell phone, but the call went right to voice mail.

Again.

Now he was worried.

He'd been by the shelter only to learn about Jessica's plan to pack up her house. But Danielle had also told him Jessica had been gone all afternoon. It wasn't like her to be out of touch with the shelter.

He'd decided to drive by her house to make certain she was okay and to let her know he was okay, as well. Robert's tactics wouldn't work. He wouldn't play those games with him.

His gut clenched when he saw the police cars parked in front of Jessica's house. He parked by the curb three houses down then jumped from his car, his pulse racing.

God, please let her be okay.

Part of the yard was taped off as a crime scene. Forensic personnel were walking to and from the house with evidence boxes and equipment. A small group of neighbors huddled on the lawn speaking to an officer, and another officer guarded the entrance.

He hesitated at the curb, torn. He wanted to see Jessica, but the thought of all the bad things that could have happened to her ran through his head. He repeated his plea to God.

Please let her be okay.

He tried to keep his voice calm as he approached the uniformed guard. "What happened here?"

"I'm going to have to ask you to step back, sir. This is a crime scene."

He pulled out his A.D.A. identification and showed it to the patrolman. It always got him into crime scenes. "I want to speak to the lead detective."

The prosecutor side of him took charge, which was good. He needed to get into that house to see what had happened and get some information about Jessica. And he didn't want the standard line they gave friends and family when something really bad happened. He wanted the truth. He routinely dealt with the police and knew being a crazy, emotional boyfriend was the best way to be escorted from the scene. Prosecutor guy would get him the answers he needed.

"Jennings."

He looked up to see Margo standing on the porch.

She sighed then waved him in. "Come on."

He went under the tape and climbed the porch steps. "Margo, what happened here? Where is Jessica? Is she all right?" And, suddenly, he was the crazy, emotional boyfriend.

She held up her hands to stop his questioning. "Jessica is okay. Paramedics transported her to the hospital. She has some bruises and probably a concussion, but she's going to be fine."

"What happened?"

"Someone pushed their way into the house and attacked Jessica. Mia ran when she realized what was happening and got a neighbor who called it in. When the first unit arrived, they found Jessica unconscious on the floor."

Andrew glanced into the living room. Overturned furniture suggested a struggle. "She fought him."

"Of course she did. I taught her that. We collected skin samples from beneath her fingernails, and there were several blood samples on the carpet."

His mind immediately went to Robert—and Sarah. "Who did this, Margo?"

"We haven't determined a suspect yet. Mia didn't see the assailant. Hopefully Jessica can tell us when she wakes up."

"But you must have a suspicion."

"It looks like a robbery gone bad. Several items are missing, her laptop included."

Robert was an opportunist. What's robbery compared to assault and possibly murder? "Is there any evidence of more than one assailant?"

"Possibly, but it's too early to tell." She must have seen where his thoughts were headed. "Andrew, there's no evidence to suggest Robert and Sarah were involved."

"It's pretty coincidental, don't you think? On the same night he has me arrested, Jessica is attacked and robbed?"

"Coincidences don't make cases. Evidence does. Now, why don't you go so we can do our job and collect that evidence?"

He was torn again between his longing to see Jessica, to make sure for himself that she was really all right, and his need to stay and make sure everything was done by the book. Robert couldn't be allowed to get away with this because of a technicality. But hadn't Bill told him that any case he was involved in would contaminate the case? Would Robert get away with this, too?

Margo must have seen the conflict in him—or maybe

she really just wanted him gone—because she touched his arm and her voice softened.

"Andrew, I had to leave Jessica in order to come back here and oversee the crime scene. I would feel better if someone she cares about was there with her when she awoke."

He thought of Jessica lying alone and hurt in the hospital. His heart broke at the image. He should be with her.

"We really do have this under control. This is what I do, Jennings." She flashed him that cocky grin he'd come to know in the time since he'd met her. She understood the conflict he was feeling. She was probably feeling it too, wanting to be with her friend but drawn to the scene to make sure whoever did this paid the price. She was giving him a way out with dignity, and he was thankful for it.

"I'll be at the hospital if you need me."

He started off the porch, but her hand on his arm tightened. He turned back to her.

"If she wakes up, you'd better call me. I mean it, Jennings."

He saw in her eyes the seriousness of that statement. She was not a lady to be trifled with. "I will."

He stepped off the porch and headed to his car. Margo went back inside and he overheard her barking orders to be careful in collecting the evidence. He reached his car and slid into the driver's seat. Despite their past encounters, he realized he liked Margo, and he was glad Jessica had a friend like her on her side.

Andrew braced himself before entering the room. His mind kept going back to all the times he'd seen Sarah beaten and bruised. It always tore at him, every single time. Now, he had to see Jessica that way, too.

He took a deep, steadying breath then pushed open the door. He took a few steps toward the bed. His breath caught in his throat when he saw her face, bruised and swollen. He held her hand and kissed it then smoothed her hair. She didn't deserve this. She shouldn't even have been involved. It was because of him and Sarah that she was here, beaten and bruised. She might say it was a risk of her job, but that didn't change the facts. She was here because he'd let her into his life.

His legs gave out and he fell to his knees. He put his face on the bed, fighting the onslaught of emotions that pelted him—anger, confusion, blind fury at the injustice of it all. He wanted to scream, cry and smash something all at once. And, most of all, he wanted Robert's head on a platter. It wasn't right that he could get away with this again and again. When did it end? When would the law finally work for justice for Sarah and Jessica and him?

Never. The police can't do anything. It's up to you to stop him.

He found himself nodding along, agreeing with his own bitter, cynical thoughts. Andrew had devoted his life to the law, and it had now failed him multiple times. Maybe it was time to take matters into his own hands. Someone had to stop Robert. If he had to be that someone, then he would.

Vengeance is mine, saith the Lord. That verse in Romans 12 wriggled its way past his bitter tirade and planted itself in his consciousness. How many times had he heard that verse echo in his mind since this mess with Sarah started? And how many times had he pushed away that promise of God's ultimate justice?

He closed his eyes and fought the primal scream that threatened to escape him. Instead, he lowered his head and directed his pleas toward Heaven. *Why, God? Why*

*is this happening again? Why does Robert seem to get
away with everything while those I love pay the price
for his actions?*

Jessica squeezed his hand and began to squirm. He
glanced at her just as she opened her eyes and looked his
way. A slight smile played on her lips when she saw him.
"Hi." Her voice was raspy and strained and, although it
tore at him to hear it like that, her voice was like music
to his ears.

"Hi. How do you feel?"

"Sore, but not too bad considering."

"You're going to be fine." He pulled her hand to his
lips and kissed it again. A new emotion—thankfulness—
pushed its way to the forefront. "I thought I'd lost you
there for a moment."

"It takes more than that to get rid of me. Ha-ha." She
tried to laugh but grimaced in pain instead, causing Andrew to leap to his feet.

"Try not to talk." He gently kissed her forehead then
pulled out his phone. "I'd better call Margo. She vowed
she'd do me bodily harm if I didn't call her when you re-
gained consciousness." He gave Jessica a playful smile.
"I believe she'd do it, too."

Margo answered on the first ring. "Hello."

"It's Andrew. She's awake." He heard what sounded
like an elevator ding.

"I'm already at the hospital. I'm on my way up now."

He closed the phone and turned back to Jessica. "She's
on her way up."

Margo entered the room and, although she kept her
calm composure, Andrew saw the worry on her face. She
tried to hide it behind a big smile.

"Girl, you look like you picked a fight with a beehive.
How do you feel?"

"I'm sore, but I'm okay." Jessica tried to sit up and both Andrew and Margo rushed to help her.

Margo played with a wisp of Jessica's hair then pulled a chair close to the bedside. "Do you remember what happened?"

Jessica nodded. "They pushed their way inside." She looked at him and his heart fell. "It was Robert and Sarah."

He didn't think his world could crumble any more, but it did. Sarah was involved. How could his Sarah get involved in hurting Jessica, who'd done nothing but try to help her?

"We have to find them. I think Sarah is in danger."

"You're right about that," Margo said, staring straight at Andrew with a hard stare. "When I get my hands on her… Nobody messes with my friend. I don't care whose sister she is."

Andrew understood her anger. "Sarah made her choice. She'll have the pay the consequences."

Jessica reached for both their hands. "No, Sarah is in danger. We have to help her."

"Jessica, honey, she attacked you."

"No, she didn't. She tried to stop Robert. Believe me, she's in trouble if she stays with that man."

Margo pulled out her cell phone. "I'll have someone go by Robert's house. If they're there, they'll be arrested."

Andrew glanced at her. "You're not going yourself?"

"I think it's better if I don't."

He saw her restraint. She was fighting the same feelings he was. "You're right. If I got my hands on him right now, I'd kill him and not give it a second thought."

A puzzled expression clouded Jessica's face. "What's wrong? Are you in pain?"

"I don't…there was someone else there."

"At the house?"

"Yes, I'm sure of it. I just can't seem to remember who. Everything is so fuzzy."

"Maybe it was the neighbor who called 911."

She shrugged. "Maybe. I can almost see his face. He spoke to me."

He rubbed her hand. "I'm sure it will come back to you, Jessica. Even if it doesn't, what does it matter?"

"It feels important, like it's something I need to remember."

Margo's phone beeped before she could make the call. She glanced at the screen then frowned and gave Andrew a strange look. "I have to go."

"Is something wrong?" Jessica asked her.

"Just work stuff." She planted a kiss on Jessica's head. "I'll check in on you later."

Andrew followed her to the door and stopped her before she walked out. "What's going on? Does this have to do with whoever broke into Jessica's house?"

"No, it's another case. A young girl Jessica was trying to help. Amy Vance."

"I know her. That's my case."

"Then you should probably come with me."

"Why? What happened? Did Shroud beat her up again?"

"No." Margo sighed. "This time he killed her."

Andrew scanned the room. Blood splattered the walls. Crime scene cones were in several spots around the floor. Photographers were still photographing and bagging evidence.

"A 911 call was placed at 10:27 p.m. Officers responded and found the body. They arrested Michael

Shroud an hour later. He had blood on his clothes and he'd recently fired a weapon."

"Did he say anything when he was arrested?"

"Yes. He said he's innocent."

He shook his head as he glanced around at the violence Michael Shroud was capable of. He'd seen violence before but it had never hit him this hard.

Worry clouded Margo's face. "I want you to ask for this case. Make sure you get it. You know, Andrew. You understand the domestic violence cycle now. Shroud is going to claim he didn't do this. He's going to try to say someone else broke in and shot her. I don't want to see him get away with murder. I want you to make sure you get justice for this young girl."

He looked around and sighed. He did know, and there was no doubt in his mind Michael Shroud was responsible.

He leaned down and stared at Amy's still, lifeless body. His heart ached for this young girl and all she'd been through.

Why? Why hadn't she allowed Jessica to help her?

He stopped by his apartment to grab the Michael Shroud case file. He'd brought it home to study even though Bill had nixed any further prosecution. That would change now. No one else had believed it merited prosecuting. Shroud had proved them all wrong.

Andrew arrived at the police station and was ushered into an interrogation room. Through the two-way mirror he saw Michael Shroud on the other side being grilled by one of the police detectives.

Andrew signed the necessary papers to hold him on murder charges. Tomorrow morning he would formally file the notice of intent to prosecute.

Michael Shroud would pay for what he'd done to Amy Vance, but this shouldn't have happened. She should have been protected before it turned to murder.

The image of her still, lifeless body wouldn't leave Andrew. He was tired of men like Shroud getting away with anything and everything, using their strength and power to terrorize and murder women.

His phone beeped indicating he had a text message. His gut clenched when he saw Sarah's number on the screen.

Help me, Andrew. I'm in trouble.

Despite what she'd done by leaving with Robert and the attack on Jessica, she was still his sister and he needed to know she was safe. He texted her back.

Where are you?

Dalton Lake. Please come get me. I'm alone and I'm scared.

Dalton Lake? A good hour's drive. How had she gotten there?

Where's Robert?

Gone. I'm alone. Please come get me.

His mind switched gears, shifting from Amy and Shroud to Sarah and Robert. How could Sarah have gone back to him after all he'd done? After all Jessica had done to help her? He didn't understand her decision, but after all he'd seen, he couldn't give up on her. He wouldn't give up on her. He had to try to help her whether she wanted it or not…before she suffered the same fate as Amy.

He was pulled. He needed to go check on Sarah, but he couldn't leave Jessica alone at the hospital. He phoned the hospital room and Mia answered.

"Andrew, don't worry. I'll stay with her," she said once Andrew explained the situation. "Besides, the pain medicine is making her sleep. You'll probably be back before she even wakes up."

He felt better knowing Mia was there with her and that she wouldn't wake up to an empty room. And besides, she was safe while Sarah might still be in trouble if Robert returned. He knew what Jessica would want him to do.

He had to go get Sarah.

"Tell her I'll be back as soon as I can."

Andrew hesitated when he saw Robert's white pickup parked by a cluster of trees. The driver's door was standing open. He parked beside it, got out and scanned the area. Sarah's message had said Robert was gone. Had she stolen his truck and fled out here? Or was Robert lying in wait for him?

He didn't see anyone else around so he walked over to the truck's open door and peered inside.

Nothing.

He touched the hood of the truck. It was still warm.

He moved toward the trees and softly called her name. "Sarah? Sarah, where are you? It's Andrew."

He heard rustling in the trees ahead of him so he moved that way. "Sarah? Is that you?"

A man stepped out from behind a tree and swung at him with something hard and metallic. Pain burst through his head and Andrew fell. His gaze grew blurry and he saw a man approach him.

Andrew held out his hand trying to steady his gaze. The man didn't look familiar. Was this a misunderstanding? Where was Sarah?

"Wait, I'm only looking for my sister."

The man leaped his way and punched him again.

Andrew fell to the ground. "I don't know you, man. I don't know what you want."

He grabbed Andrew by the shirt and yanked him up. "What I want, Counselor, is you out the picture."

"Wait! Who are you?"

"Tell Jess I'm coming for her next. She can't escape from me. She's mine and she always will be."

He punched Andrew again and this time everything went black.

Andrew woke up in his car, his head throbbing and his vision fuzzy. He glanced around at the controls, at first unable to recall what had happened or how he'd gotten into his car. The last thing he remembered was some hulk beating the tar out of him. And he'd said something about Jessica, something about coming after Jessica next.

His mind went on full alert. Jessica was in danger.

He felt around for his keys, finding them on the console. He shoved the key into the ignition and jerked the car into Reverse.

He had to get back to Jessica. He had to warn her about this guy coming after her. He searched for his phone but couldn't find it. Where had he had it last? Had he taken it out of the car when he'd gone looking for Sarah?

Sarah!

What had happened to his sister? Why hadn't she been there?

He slammed on the brakes and shifted into Park. He had to find his phone. It had to be in the car somewhere.

He felt under the seats and dug through the console. Where could it be? Had it slipped from his pocket when that man attacked him?

He glanced around at the scenery and realized he was no longer at Dalton Lake. How had he gotten back into his car? And why didn't he remember driving here?

He reached under the passenger's seat still searching for his phone. Bingo! He made contact with a solid object, grabbed hold and pulled it out then dropped it on the seat.

A knife.

A knife with blood on it.

A bloody knife in his car. This wasn't good.

Over the pounding of his heart and his head, he heard the distinct sound of sirens growing closer. A moment later, five police cars surrounded his vehicle and they jumped out, weapons drawn and aimed right at him.

"Put your hands where we can see them, Jennings!"

I want you out of the picture, Counselor.

Tell Jess I'm coming for her next.

Was this the man's plan all along? To have him surrounded by police in the hopes he would be shot and killed?

He'd watched this episode play out multiple times. The men on the force were trained to take all precautions to keep from using lethal force, and he wasn't going to give them any reason to have to.

He opened the door, raised his hands where they could be clearly seen and stepped away from his car as commanded.

Two officers ran at him, shoving him to the ground with a knee to the back, yanking his hands behind him and cuffing him.

"Andrew Jennings, you're under arrest for murder.

You have the right to an attorney. If you cannot afford an attorney…"

As another officer bagged the bloody knife that now contained his fingerprints, Andrew briefly wondered who it was he had supposedly killed.

Jessica strained to remember the attack. There was something important she'd forgotten. She was certain of it. Why couldn't she put her finger on what it was?

"How are you?"

Jessica jumped at Margo's question. She hadn't seen Margo enter the room.

"It's about time. I've been calling both you and Andrew for hours." Margo glanced around. "Where is Andrew? I thought he was coming back up here."

"I don't know. He was gone when I woke up. Mia said he called and had an errand to run."

Jessica smiled. "Admit it. You like him."

"Do not."

"Do, too. You like Andrew."

Margo shot her a look. "Yeah, well, you love him."

Jessica's breath caught. *Love* was such a strong word. How did she even know? There was a time when she'd thought she loved Mitch. "I do not love him." Yet hadn't she thought differently when Robert and Sarah had broken into her house, when she'd faced the possibility of never seeing him again?

"Yeah you do. I can tell." Margo's phone buzzed at her hip and she grabbed it and looked at the screen, a frown forming on her face.

"What's wrong?"

"I know where Andrew is." Margo sighed. "Apparently, your boyfriend just murdered Robert Young."

TEN

Staying at the hospital hadn't been an option. She wasn't going to sit there while someone she cared for was in trouble. Margo must have seen the determination in her face because she didn't protest. Instead, she instructed the nurse to bring the papers for Jessica to leave against medical advice then she grabbed Jessica's bag and pulled the car around.

"The sheriff's office made the arrest," Margo explained once they were in the car and on their way. "He's being held there."

"Can you get us in to see him?"

Margo hesitated. "Are you sure you want to see him?"

"Of course I want to see him. He didn't do this. I know he didn't. He's a good man."

Margo looked skeptical, but Jessica knew it in her heart. Andrew wasn't a violent person. It broke her heart to have people think he could be like one of those men that surrounded her every day. He was better than that. He was a good, kind Christian man with nothing in his heart but protecting his sister.

Her mind went straight to Dean. He too had been a good man, but she'd seen the hatred in his eyes when he talked about Mitch. She saw that same depth of anger sometimes in Andrew's face. *Was* it possible he'd finally snapped and taken matters into his own hands as Margo suggested?

They entered the sheriff's office and Margo led her to the waiting area.

"I'll go see what I can find out."

Jessica chewed on her fingernail as the seconds turned to minutes. Waiting was torture. Where was Margo and why hadn't she returned? She sifted through the events of the past week and realized things had gone from bad to worse. Now Andrew was accused of murder. How much worse could anything get?

She took a deep breath and tried to calm down, tried to remember that God was in this. Andrew was innocent and would soon be exonerated. The evidence would prove he couldn't have done this.

And if the evidence proved he had?

She pushed that thought away. She'd looked into the eyes of killers and seen their evil intentions. Andrew wasn't a killer.

A side door opened and Andrew appeared in handcuffs being led by two deputies.

"Andrew!" Jessica got up and ran to him, throwing her arms around his neck.

"I didn't do this, Jessica. I didn't kill Robert."

She stared up into his eyes and knew it was the truth. "I believe you."

"Someone is setting me up, Jessica. He said he wanted me out of the way. He said he was coming for you. You're in danger."

She was in danger? "Who was it?"

"I don't know, but he said, 'Tell Jess I'm coming for her next.'"

Jess? No one called her that name. No one knew her

by that name except for Margo…well, Margo and one other person.

"Let's go," one of the deputies said, prodding him to move.

"Be careful, Jessica."

She watched until they disappeared into a room and the door shut behind them. She chewed nervously on her nail again. It couldn't possibly have been Mitch. He was still in prison in Georgia.

Wasn't he?

It had been nearly two weeks since she'd checked the website. Maybe checking again wouldn't be a bad thing.

Another detective got up from his desk without logging out of his computer and she snuck over and pulled up the internet. She typed in the website address then the inmate number. Mitch's pictures loaded but at the bottom of the page his status had been updated.

Escaped.

The air left her lungs and Jessica gripped the desk for support. Mitch was out. He'd escaped, and he'd come after Andrew.

Margo rushed to her. "What are you doing? You can't be on that computer." She glanced at the screen. "Why are you looking up details of our escaped prisoner?"

Jessica glanced up at her. "Our escaped prisoner?"

"This is the guy we've been on the lookout for. Mitch Reynolds."

Jessica felt sick. Margo had told her about an escaped convict in the area, but she'd never heard the man's name, never dreamed it could be him. She pushed to her feet. Mitch had been out for days. He'd been watching her. He'd been following her. He knew about Andrew and he knew about the shelter. Everyone she knew, everyone she cared about was in danger.

Suddenly the clomping of boots shook her memory. Memories from yesterday's attack rushed through. The boots, the sneer, the look.

Mitch!

Margo grabbed her arm. "Jessica, do you know this man?"

She turned to her friend and with a heavy heart finally told her the truth. "He's the man who murdered my brother, and now he's going to kill me, too."

Andrew had sat in these interrogation rooms many times before but never as a suspect. His mind swam with all that had happened to him in the past few hours. Had he been so preoccupied with worrying over Sarah that he'd failed to see the trap set for him?

He'd only been responding to Sarah's text message, but she hadn't been the one waiting for him at Dalton Lake. Where was she? And how was she involved with this man who'd threatened Jessica?

His leg twitched nervously as his mind worked, processing all the information. This mystery man had obviously killed Robert and was framing him to make it look as if he'd been the one to murder Robert. He was doing a good frame job, too. So far, he'd managed to get Andrew to the scene, make it look as if a fight took place and had the police find him with the murder weapon… with his fingerprints on the knife.

But what did this guy want with Jessica? Knowing her, she'd probably been helping his wife or girlfriend escape him. Whatever the reason, Jessica's life was in danger, which meant he had to get out of here in order to protect her.

That wouldn't be easy since they'd locked him in this

room to stew awhile. It was a common technique and one
he knew the police used often.

Finally, the door opened but it wasn't the detectives
who entered.

It was Bill. The grim look on his face told Andrew he
was not happy. He dropped a file onto the table and folded
his arms. "When I told you to fix this matter with your
brother-in-law this wasn't what I had in mind, Andrew."

"I'm being set up."

"I'm sorry, Andrew, but I can't make this go away.
I've assigned CJ to prosecute and I've instructed her not
to go easy on you just because you're one of us. I don't
want any indications of favoritism within the D.A.'s office. I've reassigned all of your cases and as of this moment you're on personal leave."

"Whatever happened to innocent until proven guilty?"

Bill only smirked at that then opened the door.

CJ entered right after Bill walked out. She was ac-
companied by a uniformed officer. "Andrew, you know
as well as I do that our state doesn't have a manslaughter
charge. Given the circumstances, I have no choice but to
charge you with murder. I am willing, however, to offer
you a plea agreement."

He sat back in his chair and studied her. She wasn't
the sympathetic type. She was trying to be slick only he
wasn't buying her act. "You haven't even had enough
time to process the evidence. Don't you think a plea is
premature?"

She opened the file and peered at him from above her
glasses. "The victim, Robert Young, was your brother-
in-law. Married to your sister, Sarah. He was recently arrested for beating her. Subsequently you were involved
in an altercation with the deceased. Your girlfriend iden-

tified him as the man who broke into her home and assaulted her. Sounds like motive to me."

"You're drawing conclusions. You have no real evidence."

"I can convict you on this alone. You and I both know
it. And I have no doubt the physical evidence will back
me up, especially this one." She tossed the bloody knife,
now bagged and tagged onto the table.

His mind swirled. How could he get her to understand
he was being set up? Would she believe him, or simply
believe it was a ploy? How many times had he heard a
suspect declare he was being set up?

Too many times.

She stood and gathered her papers. "Get comfortable,
Counselor. You're going to be here for a while."

How had Mitch found her without her knowing he was
free? What was he doing out? And why hadn't she been
notified of his escape?

Her head was spinning at the idea that he was really
here, really out. Every sound in the busy police department was multiplied as Jessica came to grips with what
this meant for her. Every ring of the telephone was the
hiss of his voice. *You're mine, Jess.* Every reflection in
the windows was him jumping out at her, and every face
that passed by her seat was a potential threat.

She hugged her shoulders and rocked to calm the fear
that was bubbling up inside of her. Mitch was back, had
been back in her life for nearly two weeks without her
realizing it. Had it actually been Robert stalking her...
or had it been Mitch all along?

She remembered the note on her window. He'd been
that close.

The car that had run her off the road.

The broken porch light at her home.

Mrs. Brady's murder.

She gasped as she realized Mitch had been there, watching her all along. Tears fell on her cheek as she realized Mrs. Brady had suffered at Mitch's hands. And Robert…?

She glanced at the hallway where Andrew had been led away in handcuffs. Mitch had killed Robert and framed Andrew for the murder. But why? She sighed. She knew why. Mitch had seen Andrew with her and wanted him out of the way.

After what seemed like hours, Margo emerged from the hallway and motioned to Jessica. She got up and rushed over.

"What's happening?" she asked. "Where is Andrew?"

"Follow me."

Margo opened the door to an interrogation room and ushered her inside. In her hand, she held a file. Andrew, now free from the handcuffs, stood when she entered. Jessica rushed to him and hugged him tightly.

"Have a seat." Margo pulled a chair over and motioned for Jessica to sit down before removing a photograph from the file folder in her hand. She tossed it across the table.

Andrew pulled it toward him then nodded. "That's him. That's the man that attacked me and set me up."

He pushed the photo to Jessica. She didn't dare touch it. She didn't need to. Mitch's cold blue eyes glared at her from his prison photo.

"He escaped from the Georgia State Correctional Facility three weeks ago. The FBI recently expanded the search to include our area due to some very sketchy possible sightings."

"Does he have a connection here?"

"None that we knew of—" she glanced at Jessica "—until now."

Andrew turned to look at her, too. "Who is this man? How does he know you?"

She stared at him and knew it was time to come clean about Mitch and her past. Now, he would finally know the truth about her. She wasn't just like one of those women she counseled. She was one of them.

She turned the photo over so that Mitch's eyes were no longer probing into her. "He wants me. It's always been about me. Mitch stalked and terrorized me for weeks. Dean tried to protect me from him."

"And Reynolds killed him?"

"Yes." The memory of that night was forever seared in her mind. Mitch had nearly killed her, as well. It was only the timely arrival of the police that had saved her life.

"But why is he after you? Did you help his wife or his girlfriend?"

She stared at Andrew and felt her heart tear inside of her. He still saw her as the woman she pretended to be, the one who helped others out of trouble instead of the one who needed help. "No." She opened her mouth to tell him, but the words died on her lips. This confession would forever change their relationship.

"Did you witness one of his crimes? Is that why he's after you?" He sighed, exasperated with her. "Jessica, what is your connection to this monster?"

"It's a personal connection." Margo glanced her way. "Isn't it?"

Tears spilled down her face. She nodded and wiped them away. "I was twenty-two when I met Mitch Reynolds. We dated for eight months. I didn't know what kind of man he was at first, but it didn't take long before he revealed his true self. When I tried to break up with him, he—" her voice caught "—he became violent. Dean was only trying to help me, but Mitch stabbed Dean. He murdered him."

"So he escapes from prison and comes to find you. He's obsessed with you," Margo said.

She nodded. "He always told me I belonged to him and that no one or nothing would ever separate us."

Margo let out a sigh of aggravation. "Why didn't you ever tell me?"

"I didn't want to burden you."

"You were in danger, Jessica. You should have told me. You should have trusted me."

Margo was right. She should have told someone, but she'd naively believed that part of her life was behind her. Despite the fear she'd carried around, she had never really believed she would ever be in this situation again.

Or maybe she had believed it. Maybe that was why she'd kept everyone at arm's length for so long.

Margo picked up the file and walked out, slamming the door as she left. Jessica jumped at such a loud indicator of her anger. She wiped at the tears streaming down her face. Margo deserved better than she'd given her. She'd been a much better friend than Jessica had.

Andrew reached out and held her hand in his. When she looked up into his face, his expression was not one of condemnation, but of compassion and understanding. "She'll calm down. She's just hurt that you didn't trust her."

"I should have. I owed her more than that."

He squeezed her hand. "I wish you'd trusted me enough to tell me the truth, but I don't blame you. The police will capture him and everything will be fine."

"Until when? Until he escapes again? I thought I was

safe while he was in prison, but I wasn't. I'll never be safe from him."

"You're not alone in this. We'll get through this together. I won't let him hurt you, Jessica."

Pain like a knife twisted in her heart. She'd already witnessed Andrew's protective nature with Sarah. He would try to protect her, too. She couldn't allow that... Wouldn't allow that. Mitch had already done so much damage—Andrew had been accused of murder, disgraced as a prosecutor. She couldn't let him risk his life, as well.

"I can't let you get involved in this. It's too dangerous. Mitch is too dangerous."

"Too late. I'm already involved. I won't let him hurt you."

"It's not you he wants. It's me."

"You don't have to go through this alone."

"Don't I? I brought this on. People are dead because of me, Andrew, because I was foolish enough to believe Mitch's lies. I won't let anyone else pay the price for my foolishness."

She got up to leave, but he stood and blocked her way. "If you think you can get rid of me that easily then you're wrong. I'm not leaving you to face this man alone."

"Don't you understand? Mitch will kill anyone I'm close to."

"I'm not afraid of him."

The image of Dean stepping in front of her, the knife plunging into his chest, flashed through her mind. "You should be. He's dangerous."

"I will not give up on you, Jessica, and I will not let you push me away. I don't care what happened in your past. I only care about your future...our future." He reached for her hand and held her. "I love you too much to let you face this alone."

Her heart skipped a beat. Had he just proclaimed his love for her? That knife turned another round.

He pressed closer. "Did you hear me? I said I love you. I want to spend my life with you, Jessica."

Tears filled her eyes. She pulled her hand away and walked to the door. "I'm sorry. I don't have a life to give you."

She knocked on the door and thankfully someone opened it. She rushed out before he could protest further.

The tears she'd been holding back burst through. With Mitch roaming free, nothing would ever be fine again.

What was happening? His world seemed to be crumbling around him. Andrew paced the small jail cell where they'd placed him. His mind was working through every detail he could remember. He'd responded to a text message from Sarah only to walk into a trap.

So where was Sarah? Had this Mitch Reynolds hurt her? He bit back that bitter pill. Better not to think that way. Maybe Sarah had escaped, dropping her phone in the process. She couldn't call for help and she was alone.

He gripped the bars and pushed against them, anything to work out the agitation. Two women he loved were in trouble and he'd been stuck inside a jail cell for nearly twenty-four hours where there was nothing he could do.

He leaned against the bars. Nothing he could do but pray.

God?

He gulped away the panic that threatened him. He'd once believed in an all-powerful God, one who could protect those he loved. But He hadn't protected Tory. Why should Andrew give Him a second chance?

He sat down on the bed. What else could he do? Where else could he turn? He was at his lowest and there was no one else to turn to.

"Andrew."

He looked up to see Margo standing there.

"Margo, where is Jessica? Is she safe?"

"She's fine. She's gone back to the shelter. I've got a call in to a couple of off-duty friends to act as security guards at the shelter."

"What about Sarah? Has anyone heard from her? Does he have her?"

"Calm down, Andrew. Sarah is okay. We issued a bulletin for both her and Robert's cars. A patrol car found her walking down Littleton Street. She's beat up, but she's fine."

"Can I see her?"

She nodded then motioned to someone down the hallway. Moments later a uniformed officer led Sarah in.

He looked up and saw Sarah running down the hallway. Tom was behind her. Margo unlocked the cell and Sarah rushed into his arms.

He hugged her tightly, relief flooding him. "Are you all right? Are you hurt?"

"I'm fine," she assured him. Tears flooded her eyes. "I figured after the way we left it that I couldn't call you anymore for help. I'm sorry, Andrew. I shouldn't have left Jessica's. I should have listened to you."

He pulled her into hug. "You can always call me, Sarah. It doesn't matter how angry I get, I'll always be there to help you."

"We need to take her statement," Margo said.

Andrew nodded and released her. Sarah was safe. That was all that mattered. And with Robert dead, she would stay safe.

Margo motioned toward an officer who escorted Sarah out.

"I'll be in shortly to represent her," Tom said.

Margo nodded then walked off.

Tom quickly got down to business. Andrew had called him in once he realized the mess he was in. "I'm challenging the legality of the search of your vehicle. It was predicated only on an anonymous tip, certainly not enough for probable cause. The knife is tainted evidence. Don't worry. You'll be out by tomorrow."

Tomorrow might be too late. "What about bail?"

"CJ told me she would be asking for high bail."

"I don't care what it costs. I'll pay whatever I have to as long as it gets me out today."

Knowing Sarah was safe should have helped ease the urgency he felt, but it didn't. The danger was still out there lurking around, looking for an opportunity to strike. And he was helplessly stuck here.

"Please, Tom. See what you can do. Jessica is in trouble, and a madman has taken extreme measures to keep me out of the way."

Tom nodded and picked up his briefcase. "Okay. I'll go see what I can do about getting you out of here tonight."

After Andrew wrote a big fat check to the city clerk's office, Tom pushed open the courthouse door and led the way as Andrew followed. "Keep your head down and don't say anything." The group of reporters crowding the courthouse steps pounced the moment they were through the doors, shoving cameras and microphones in his face and shouting questions.

"Andrew, why did you kill your brother-in-law?"

"Did you think you could get away with it because of your position in the D.A.'s office?"

"Did he threaten you?"

He slipped on his sunglasses and pushed his way past them, ignoring their questions.

He reached Tom's sedan and slid into the passenger's seat as Tom got behind the wheel. A reporter banged on the window, the questions continuing through the glass. "Why did you do it?"

He turned his head away from the camera lens as Tom started the engine and put the car in gear. There was a time when he'd craved the attention of the press. Now he'd give anything to make them go away.

Oh, how his life had changed.

"So what do you want to do now?" Tom asked as they left the crowd behind them.

He took a deep breath. Only one thing occupied his mind. "I have to see Jessica."

"After what you went through with Tory, I have to ask," Tom stated. "Are you sure getting involved with Jessica is a good idea? The risks—"

"Are necessary," Andrew finished. "I've been with her, Tom. She doesn't seek out danger, but she doesn't run from it either, not when it means keeping others safe."

"And you're okay with that?"

"I'm better than okay with it," Andrew said, smiling. "It's the main reason I fell in love with her."

You're mine, Jess.

She jerked awake, those words haunting her dream. She was still at her desk, having fallen asleep some time during making phone calls. How could she sleep knowing the mess she'd made? She checked the security feed and saw the two off-duty police officers Margo had found to act as security guards still up front. The women were somewhat safe for now, but she had to clear the shelter.

Those officers would be no match for Mitch if he really wanted to get inside. Jessica knew he would harm anyone and everyone who got in his way.

Her mind was already again working, going over plans, people she could call, things that needed to be taken care of. She'd called every shelter within a hundred miles looking for available beds, but she was having trouble finding enough. But it was time to start moving out the ladies that she had found a place for.

She couldn't abandon these women, but she couldn't let them stay here with Mitch nearby. He wouldn't hesitate to use any one of them to get to her.

She forced her legs to stand and walked toward the kitchen, needing coffee. She walked by the common room and found several of the women standing around the television. The news was on talking about Andrew and the women were shaking their heads in disbelief.

"Assistant District Attorney Andrew Jennings was in court this morning for his preliminary hearing on charges of murder."

Jessica looked up at the television screen as a video of Andrew leaving the courthouse ran. He was surrounded by lights and flashes and screaming reporters, all hollering at him for a chance to tell his story. She'd seen him play up for the camera before, his handsome face always a plus for him, but today he lowered his face and rushed past them without commenting.

The newscaster continued. "A.D.A. Jennings is known to be tough on crime on those whose cases he prosecutes. But now the city is wondering will the D.A.'s office be tough on this crime?"

She walked over and switched off the television. "Why are you all standing around watching this instead of packing?"

Deloris stepped forward. "Honey, what's going on? He seemed like such a nice young man. I'm sure this is a mistake."

Mia appeared in the doorway and called to her. "Jessica, I thought you were sleeping."

She frowned at Mia. "I don't have time for sleeping. Why didn't you wake me?"

"I-I thought you needed the rest."

She stopped and turned to the girl, realizing how young and innocent she really was. "You don't seem to understand. We have to clear out this shelter as soon as possible. We're still short two beds. I'm going to call some friends in Shreveport and see if they can put up Joan and Deloris. I need you to make sure the rest of the ladies are packed and ready to go as soon as possible."

"You're scaring me, Jessica."

"You should be scared, Mia. Until this place is cleared out, we're all in danger."

Mia reluctantly nodded then scurried away.

Jessica went to the kitchen and saw the coffeepot was empty. She'd been through two entire pots of coffee already in the past twenty-four hours. Her body ached to rest, but she couldn't, not until everyone was safely away from her. These women had enough danger to worry about without piling hers on top of their situations. They would be taken care of in other shelters. And Jessica had even managed to find a home for Mrs. Brady's dog.

The doorbell rang and Jessica flinched. Who was coming here? And what did they want? She grabbed her coffee cup and headed down the hall. She'd given strict instructions to Mia and the other ladies not to answer the door. Not to even go near it. No one needed to be let inside without Jessica knowing about it.

She checked the security feed and saw Andrew standing on the stoop. She sighed. Why was he here? Hadn't they already said everything that needed to be said?

She set down her cup and unlocked the door, bracing herself for what she had to do. She'd known he would come and had practiced what to say to him when he did, gone over and over it in her head until she could recite every word without the tear of her heart bleeding through. This had to be believable. He had to be convinced it was over between them. She had to hurt him to save him.

His life depended on it.

She unlocked the door but the words died on her lips the moment she saw him. His green eyes glistened with pain as he looked at her. She'd never seen him so defeated and her arms ached to hold him, to offer comfort and reassurance.

Instead, she was about to knock him down another peg. Her heart screamed at her not to do it. How much more could he take?

Lord, I can't do this alone.

"What are you doing here, Andrew? I asked you not to come here. I thought I made myself clear."

"I won't abandon you, Jessica."

"I don't need your help, Andrew, and I don't want it."

"You have a madman after you."

"Which it turns out has nothing to do with you."

"It has everything to do with me. I care about you, Jessica." He stared into her eyes. "I love you."

He'd said it earlier, but her heart still soared for only a moment…that was all she could give it.

Andrew loved her.

Hurt him to save him.

Hurt him to save him.

Hurt him to save him.

She was used to staring down monsters and masking

her fear. She could do the same with love…couldn't she? She had to. She steeled herself against the overwhelming emotion that threatened to spill over.

She turned to Officer Brown standing guard by the front door. "Would you give us a minute please?"

He nodded in understanding. "I'll go get myself a cup of coffee."

When he disappeared down the hall, she turned back to Andrew. It was time to be strong.

"I'm sorry, Andrew. I never meant to give you the wrong idea."

"What do you mean?"

"I see where this is headed—a relationship—and I'm sorry but I just can't go there right now. I have responsibilities, people who depend on me. I can't allow anything or anyone to get in the way of that."

"I would never get in the way of what you do. I think you're amazing."

Her heart wrenched. It was so unfair! After all this time, after all these years, she was hearing the words she'd longed to hear for so long from a truly wonderful man and she couldn't even enjoy them.

Mitch had truly taken everything from her.

She searched for something to say, her mind coming up blank due to the wonderful daze of his declarations.

A scream from the back grabbed her attention.

Jessica took off running, Andrew right behind her. She ran toward the kitchen, sliding to a halt when she saw Officer Brown sprawled unmoving on the floor.

She peeked into the kitchen and saw Joan crouching beneath the table. "Someone's inside," she whispered, her voice grainy with panic.

Jessica felt her gut clench. Someone was inside the shelter? Mitch? Or someone else? These women were all still in danger from outside sources that had nothing to do with Mitch.

Andrew grabbed the officer's gun, still in its holster, and stepped in front of her. "I'll check it out."

She wasn't letting him go alone. She followed him through the kitchen and into the hallway leading toward her office. The door was partially open.

She gasped. Someone was in her office.

"Wait here," Andrew commanded her.

She shook her head. She wasn't leaving his side to face the danger alone.

She followed him as he pushed open her office door and surveyed the room. He turned back to her and shook his head. "I don't see anyone."

Screams still resonated through the halls. These women were scared and they had every right to be. Danger was lurking somewhere in these hallways.

"Call 911," Andrew said, handing her his cell phone.

Jessica nodded and dialed the number as Andrew moved cautiously further down the hall.

Before she could hit the send button, a loud crash grabbed her attention. She looked up to see a man step from around the corner and tackle Andrew, knocking him against the wall. The gun fell from his hand as he slid to the floor.

Jessica screamed and dropped the phone. Terror ripped through her at the sight of those broad shoulders. She recognized his frame, his stance, his presence even before he turned his steely blue eyes on her.

Mitch!

It really was him!

She turned to flee but he lunged for her, catching her ankle and dragging her down. She screamed, kicking and fighting to free herself, but she was no match for his overpowering weight.

He grabbed her chin then leaned in real close. "Happy to see me, babydoll?"

She pulled at his grip. "What do you want? Why are you here?"

"You know why, Jess. You belong to me. Never forget that."

She heard the cries of fear coming from the den over the shrill of the alarm. Those women had trusted her to keep them safe. She couldn't let Mitch take out his revenge on them. "Please don't hurt anyone. I'll do anything."

"Oh, babydoll. You'll do everything." He pulled her to her feet. "Where's the alarm control?"

"Up front by the main door."

He motioned that way. "Let's go."

"Get your hands off her now!"

Mitch turned toward her and Jessica saw Andrew still dazed but on his feet, the gun aimed toward them.

Mitch's hand tightened around her neck. "Drop the gun or I snap her neck."

He didn't flinch, and he didn't drop the gun. "Step away from her. Now!"

Mitch leaned down and whispered in Jessica's ear. "What are you going to do? You can't protect them all can you, babydoll? Someone has to suffer. Maybe I'll slit his throat like I slit Dean's."

Andrew stepped closer. "I said move!"

She fell back on the training Margo had shown her. She kicked Mitch hard in the shin then spun around and jabbed her palm into his nose. He hollered then stumbled backward, blood gushing from his face. Jessica dropped to the floor as shots rang out and Mitch fell backward.

He grabbed his shoulder then took off running out the back door.

"Are you okay?" Andrew asked as he moved toward the back door.

She nodded, but lay on the floor waiting for her heartbeat to return to normal as Andrew ran out the back after Mitch. He returned a moment later.

"He's gone."

"Jessica!" Mia rushed toward her. "Are you hurt? What can I do?"

"I'm fine," Jessica assured her. She crawled to her feet.

"I heard the commotion. I hid behind a desk. I'm so sorry, Jessica. I didn't know what to do."

"It's okay, Mia. There was nothing you could have done."

"I'm pretty sure I got him in the shoulder," Andrew said as he got up and walked to the door, closed it and locked it.

She turned to Mia. "Please go check on everyone and let them know everything is fine now."

Mia glanced at her then at Andrew before turning and leaving the room.

Jessica saw the determination in Andrew's face. He would die before he would let Mitch hurt anyone.

He would die…and Jessica just couldn't let that happen.

Hurt him to save him.

Hurt him to save him.

She pushed against the wall, needing the support for what she was about to do.

"What were you thinking, Andrew?"

"I was trying to protect you."

"I told you the day you brought Sarah here that your

form of protection is going to get someone killed. Today, that almost happened."

"He had you by the throat, Jessica."

"Yes, and your macho bravado only made the situation worse. I don't need you to take care of me. I told you before that I can take care of myself. All you did today was to put me and my girls in more danger."

"I know you're scared, but—"

"This isn't about me being scared. This is about you getting in the way. Now please leave…and don't come back. Whatever it was you thought we had between us is over." She walked away from him, her legs threatening to buckle at any moment, but she'd stood her ground.

This time, he didn't follow her.

The act of walking to his car took all the strength Andrew could muster. He didn't start the engine right away, but sat in his car, trying to grasp what had just happened. One moment, Jessica had been the only good thing left in his life, and the next, she was pushing him away and speaking daggers into him.

He closed his eyes and concentrated on his breath, ignoring the rock that was forming in the pit of his stomach. Was she really going to throw away what they had? Or had they ever really had it?

He was torn between believing she was only pushing him away because she was scared and believing she meant what she said.

He'd survived Tory's death, but how would he ever survive Jessica's departure from his life?

ELEVEN

Margo arrived at the shelter with two FBI agents in tow, a male agent who looked like he could have been a linebacker and a petite female agent.

"They're taking over the hunt for Reynolds," she told Jessica. "These are Agents Vince Robbins and Anna Warren."

Agent Robbins slammed a thick file folder onto the kitchen table. "We need to ask you a few questions, if you don't mind."

"Fine." Jessica took a seat opposite him as he flipped open the file and skimmed through it.

"I know what he did to you, Jessica. I read the file. I spoke with the detectives who worked your brother's case. I know how Reynolds tortured you. When did you learn that Reynolds had escaped?"

"Today."

"It says here the Department of Corrections made multiple attempts to contact you but didn't have your correct information." He slid a form with her contact information listed.

"That was my address in Atlanta. I updated it when I moved. I don't understand why it wasn't changed."

"Didn't you think it was odd that no one had ever contacted you about his status?"

"I've been checking the website. I checked it two weeks ago and his status hadn't changed. I had no reason to think he was out."

Margo sighed, frustrated. "Jessica, you don't check a website. You pick up the phone."

"I didn't want it to be that important. I didn't want to give him that kind of control."

"So you haven't seen him or had contact with him?" Agent Warren asked.

"No. Not until I remembered it was him who was at my house the night Robert was killed, and then tonight when he broke into the shelter."

"But you've been having some issues lately. I understand someone has been following you, leaving you notes and sending you text messages."

"I thought that was someone else." She glanced away. She had nothing to hide and the truth was the truth. "I hoped it was."

"We have a theory here. He's been watching you for a while now, Jessica. He squatted at your neighbor's house until her death was discovered. He knows where you're staying, where you work. He's obsessed with you. But he's been underground for too long. Someone must be helping him. Who would he go to Jessica?"

"I don't know."

"Does he have any other connections in town besides you?"

"I don't know. I don't think so."

"Someone must be helping him," the agent repeated.

"Well, I don't know who it is."

Agent Warren approached her. "Why did he come here, Jessica? He could have been halfway across the country. Instead, he tracked you down. He's watched you. Toyed with you. What does he want from you, Jessica?"

She stared into the kind but tough eyes of Agent Warren. "He wants me to know that he's still in control. He still holds the power. He won't give up."

"Why? What's his end game?" She slid into a chair opposite Jessica. "You're the expert here on this type of behavior. Profile this guy for us. How will this end?"

"It won't end. It will never end. As long as he has the power, he will always continue to exert control over my life. He'll use anyone and everyone in my life against me. I don't know what I did, why he's fixated on me, but he is and that won't end until one of us is dead."

"Then he does want to kill you?"

"Eventually, but not until I and everyone around me has suffered."

Robbins nodded toward his partner. "I think we should go public. Flood the area with his photograph. I don't want him to be able to go anywhere in this town without being recognized."

Agent Warren nodded her agreement. "I'll make the necessary calls." She pulled out her phone.

"I'll make arrangements for a team to dust for prints and collect evidence." He stood and closed his file. "I understand your boyfriend shot him?"

"He's not my boyfriend...but yes. There's blood by the back door."

He stood and pointed toward Mia. "Show me."

"We'll need to place you in protective custody, Jessica," Agent Warren told her. "We have safe houses where he won't be able to get to you."

"No, I'm not going anywhere."

Margo spoke up. "Jessica, listen to the FBI. Go to the safe house."

"I can't...not until my girls are safe. I'm still trying to find a place for Joan and Deloris to go. I can't leave until I know they're safe."

"I will take care of Joan and Deloris. You have to take care of yourself."

She stood her ground. "I'll go to your safe house, but I need a day, two days at most. I won't leave until they're out of harm's way."

Agent Warren must have noticed her determination because she didn't try to change her mind. "I'll make arrangements for a protection detail. We can set up here until you're ready."

Jessica nodded her agreement. "Thank you, Agent Warren."

She opened her phone and turned away.

Margo jumped to her feet, glancing at Jessica then at Agent Warren. "Are you seriously allowing this? The maniac has already broken in here once. He knows where she is. How can you allow her to stay here? She needs to be somewhere Reynolds can't find her."

"The shelter has its own safety features that we can build on for the short-term."

Margo's eyes blazed. "You're hoping he comes back here, aren't you? You're planning to use Jessica as bait."

"If he returns, we'll be ready for him." She placed her phone to her ear and walked off as an angry Margo turned to face Jessica.

"How can you let them do this to you, Jessica?"

"It won't be for long, only a day or two."

"I don't understand how you can even choose to stay here."

"Do you think I'm not terrified? I am, but I have two women in my care who rely on me to protect them. But instead of making their lives safer, I've brought dan-

ger to their doorstep. Now, I have to rectify that. I have
to place their safety before my own. I can't leave them
vulnerable."

"I can handle that."

Her voice shook but she pressed her hands against
the table and stood on unsteady legs. "You don't get it,
Margo. He's taken everything from me—my home, my
job, Andrew. Dean's Den was the culmination of my
life's dream. I sunk every dime I had from Dean's life
insurance into making this shelter work. I've poured my
heart and my soul into this place, into this mission to
help. Now, it's nearly gone and once it is, I will have
truly lost everything."

Margo stared at her then nodded, seeming to understand her need to finish this.

Jessica felt bad for not letting her friend in. "I'm sorry
I never told you about Mitch. I should have."

As usual, she shrugged off any touch of emotion. "I
guess we all have our homicidal maniacs after us, don't
we?"

Jessica grinned as she pulled her friend into a hug.
"When this is over, I want you to promise me that you'll
move on with your life. Find you a nice man and do what
normal people do. Go out to eat, see a movie, get married, have kids."

"I will if you will."

Margo's comment was offhanded and flippant, but the
truth was Jessica was thinking about how wonderful it
would be to settle down with Andrew and start a family.
And how impossible it would be.

When she didn't respond, Margo looked over and nodded knowingly. "Oh. I see. You really have been thinking about this, haven't you? It doesn't have to be over,

Jessica. You don't have to let Mitch win. Andrew loves you. You can have that life."

Oh, how she wished that were true. But that part of her life was over. Forever. "It's too late for that."

Agent Robbins reentered the kitchen. "We have a problem. There's no evidence of forced entry on the back door or on the gate. This was an inside job. Someone either let him into the building or gave him a key."

Jessica was shocked by this news. Someone she knew was helping Mitch? The FBI had seemed so certain when they'd suggested it, but Jessica had a hard time believing anyone she knew would help Mitch terrorize her.

Someone she knew had betrayed her.

Jessica helped Deloris pack her things so that they would be prepared to leave immediately once a bed opened up elsewhere. When they were finished packing, Jessica hugged her. "I'm going to miss you."

"Listen to an old woman who's wasted most of her life, Jessica. Learn to take a chance, and I don't mean risking life and limb. Honey, learn to risk your heart. Andrew is a nice man. Give him a chance. Take a risk on love."

Jessica hugged her again wishing she could take a chance on love. Mitch would make that impossible. He would never give up on her. He would never stop interfering. And he would kill anyone she loved just to hurt her.

Mia was at the front desk taking down a list.

"We're almost through here. I'll be home as soon as I can." She hung up when she saw Jessica approach.

Jessica eyed the list—gauze, bandages, antiseptic. "Is someone hurt?"

"It's John. He cut his hand chopping up some onions at my apartment. He said it's bleeding pretty good. I told him I would be home soon."

"Sure, go ahead, Mia. See about your fellow. Hopefully, my friend in Shreveport will call soon about those beds."

Mia nodded but her face was downcast. Jessica hated putting the girl out of a job, but it was better than putting her life in danger.

"What are you going to do, Jessica?" Mia asked her.

"I don't know yet, but I'll have my cell phone wherever I go. If you need me, you can call me." Jessica hugged her. "Now go and take care of your guy."

"Goodbye, Jessica." Mia walked to her car and slid inside.

She hugged herself as she watched Mia drive away. She stared at the dark, vacant building where she'd invested the past two years of her life. Tears slipped from her eyes. She was alone.

She locked the door to the shelter and went to her office. Her files were boxed and ready for storage. There would soon be no one here left to minister to or care for. She'd notified the department that she was unavailable for crisis calls until further notice and alerted them to the fact that the FBI was there protecting her.

There was nothing left to do but wait. Wait for the FBI to surround her. Wait for Mitch to try to kill her. Wait to start a new life in a new town where no one could find her.

Dean's Den was the culmination of her passion, a calling God had placed on her life. But now she had to let it go just as she'd had to break ties with Andrew. It wasn't fair.

Mitch had truly taken everything from her.

Andrew unlocked his apartment and carried in bags of groceries. As he walked inside, he noticed Sarah sitting in a corner with a book in her hands. She got up and walked over to help him unload the bags.

"What were you reading?"

"Nothing." She shrugged. "A Bible study Jessica gave me. I hope you don't mind that I borrowed your Bible to look up some verses."

His Bible? Where had she even found it? He couldn't remember the last time he'd seen it. "Where was it?"

"On the bookshelf beneath some legal thrillers. I guess you haven't read it in a while."

"No, I haven't."

"I haven't read mine, either. Maybe that's why I got so messed up. Maybe that's why you got messed up, too."

"I'm not messed up. What are you talking about?"

"Andrew, look at you. You've lost everything. You lost your job, you're scandalized and now you're heartbroken, too. It would have been better if you'd never met Jessica."

He wanted to argue with her, but with each day that passed, his heart grew heavier. She'd shut him out completely, refusing to accept his calls or see him.

He noticed his Bible still on the table by the window. He opened it, skimming through the pages. His mind needed to be occupied with something besides Jessica, besides the words she'd said to him…besides the idea that he would never hold her again. There had been a time in his life when he'd studied God's word. He'd made notes in the margins. He realized it had indeed been a long time since he'd opened this book. In fact, it had been a long time since he'd turned to God in any way.

He rubbed his hands together. Why was turning to God such a difficult feat? It wasn't, but it was hard after so long. Humbling. Jessica's image sprang to his mind and he smiled. She would understand why this was so hard for him. Hard to admit that he needed someone, even if that someone was God.

God...

Words escaped him. He couldn't even put voice to what he needed. Protection for Jessica. A future with her. His job.

What did he want to ask for?

One word—*Jessica.*

"God, help her."

He got her voice mail again.

Andrew sighed, frustrated by Jessica's lockout.

He waited for the beep then spoke into the phone. "Jessica, it's Andrew again. I wish you would talk to me. I spoke to Margo. She says Agents Robbins and Warren have the shelter on lockdown so I'm glad you're safe. I miss you. Please call me."

He put the phone away and joined Tom in the waiting area outside the conference room of the District Attorney's Office. The heavy door to the conference room was closed, a tactic used by the prosecutor's office to wire up defendants. He'd used it before and although he'd known it worked, he had no idea it worked so well.

"Calm down," Tom said.

"How can I calm down? This is my life, my career. What did CJ say when you spoke to her on the phone earlier?"

"Only that they've had new evidence come to light that would affect the case against you."

His mind soared. Her wording was carefully chosen. That could mean good or bad. Had they found something they thought further incriminated him? Or were they taking Sarah's statement as an exoneration?

The door opened and a paralegal stepped outside. "They're ready for you now."

CJ and Bill were seated behind the massive table. They both had their expressions masked. Nothing would be given away prematurely.

He and Tom sat down on the other side.

CJ pulled at the tip of her pen, clicking it. That meant she was nervous.

Bill spoke for the two. "New evidence has been presented in the death of Robert Young. As you know, Andrew, your sister was able to identify the man whose fingerprints were found in the Taylor house. Also, her statement seems reliable. No holes in her story. Plus, the evidence appears to support her statement that another man, this escaped convict the police have been searching for, entered Jessica's home and killed your brother-in-law. We don't yet know why he would do something like that. Or why he would move the body."

Andrew set his expression not willing to give away anything. He knew why Reynolds had broken into Jessica's house and killed Robert, but as far as he was concerned that was none of their business.

"However," Bill continued, "we've determined his motives have no bearing on the case against you so the District Attorney's Office—" He glanced over at CJ, who looked unhappy with the entire situation, indicating to Andrew that when Bill said the D.A.'s office, he really meant he'd made the decision. Anticipation licked Andrew's soul. This part of his nightmare was about to be over.

Bill continued "Is officially withdrawing its charges."

Relief sagged through him. At least one thing was over. "What about my job?"

Bill nodded to CJ and the paralegals. They gathered their papers and exited the room.

"There is still the matter of your behavior surrounding your brother-in-law."

"What behavior?"

"You assaulted him. That is not the kind of behavior this office wants from its personnel."

"He's dead. It won't happen again."

"What about the next time? Are you planning to assault every man your sister becomes involved with?"

"If he beats her then yes, I absolutely will."

Bill raked a hand through his hair. "Andrew, the Office of the District Attorney cannot—"

"No, Bill. This is the problem. This office does not understand or defend the rights of abused victims. As a prosecutor, I tossed aside too many cases because I believed they were unwinnable and this office, specifically you, not only agreed with those assessments, you encouraged them. We are the prosecutor's office. We are supposed to search for justice for our victims, but most of the time the victim is not even a factor in our work in this office."

"We are a government agency. We have a limited number of resources available. We prosecute what we can."

"How can we expect to change the opinions of the hearts and minds of the public if we won't stand up for domestic violence victims and proclaim that they are just as important as other victims of crime?"

"We are forced to work within the confines of the law."

"I'm not asking to circumvent the law. I'm asking for a chance to make the law work for this population of offenders and their victims. Victims like Amy Vance, one woman in a long line of women victimized by Michael

Shroud. We might have avoided her death had we intervened more intensely in the case."

Bill looked put off by his mention of the Shroud case,
a case he'd personally forced Andrew to drop.

"Andrew Jennings, you are hereby sanctioned for in-
appropriate behavior detrimental to the reputation of the
Office of the District Attorney. Your file will be noted
with this sanction. You are reinstated beginning today.
We will be releasing an official notice to the press in a
few hours." He stood to leave.

"Bill, wait. Michael Shroud?"

"I've already reassigned that case."

"I want it back. It was mine to begin with."

He nodded then left the room.

Andrew could hardly contain the grin that stretched
across his face. He'd gotten his job back and he'd also
managed to get Bill to let him prosecute Shroud. He
couldn't wait to give Jessica the good news.

He glanced at Tom, who was getting up.

"Congratulations, Andrew. You did it."

"I did. Thank you for your help, Tom. I really appreciate it."

"Glad I could help. Besides, how often do I get the
chance to be involved in such a high-profile case? It'll
probably double my client base."

Andrew smiled. There was a time in his life when that
was also how he'd equated success. "I expect you'll remember that when you're totaling my bill."

Tom grinned then turned to leave. He stopped and
turned back. "If you need any outside assistance on that
Shroud case, let me know. I'd like to help."

"Just don't take this guy on as a client."

Tom smiled. "Batterers? Even defense attorneys have
their standards, Andrew."

They walked out together. Members of the press rushed toward them, shoving microphones at them.

Tom spoke first. "The District Attorney's Office has officially exonerated my client for any wrongdoing in the death of his brother-in-law. He has also been reinstated to his old position as prosecuting attorney."

A Channel Six reporter pushed a microphone into Andrew's face. "How do you feel about being cleared of these allegations?"

His eyes scoped out the scene. It was amazing that something as unimportant to the world as his meeting with Bill Foster could produce such interest. He supposed it was a good story. It had all the elements of good television—blood, family and love.

There was a time in his life when he'd craved this much attention. He'd hungered for it. He'd based the successfulness of his life and career on this attention. Now he understood it was fleeting. It offered him no satisfaction. In fact, in the past weeks, he'd come to despise it.

But God could use him even in this. "I feel justified. I didn't kill him, but I can't say I'm sorry he's dead. This man beat and terrorized my little sister. She never got justice for what was done to her. I don't think that's right. Beginning tomorrow, I'll be the lead attorney on the Michael Shroud case. Mr. Shroud battered and killed a sweet young girl, a student of his. Her name was Amy Vance, and my sincere hope is that I can finally get justice for her and her family by putting her killer behind bars for a very long time."

Agent Warren knocked on her office door as Jessica was packing to go to the safe house. With Deloris and Joan safely relocated, she was finally prepared to go into hiding. "You should turn on the local news."

Curious, Jessica picked up the remote and hit the on button. A news conference on the steps of the courthouse showed Andrew speaking to a group of reporters and the banner across the screen announced that charges had been dropped against him.

She smiled, glad to see he was finally getting his life back. It was a good start.

The channel replayed his speech about standing up for victims like Amy Vance and Jessica's heart melted.

"He seems like a good guy," Agent Warren said.

Jessica smiled. "He's a wonderful man who didn't deserve everything that happened to him."

Agent Warren put on her official face. "We'll be leaving in two hours for the safe house. Make sure you have anything you want to take packed."

Jessica turned off the television then went back to her packing. She picked up her phone. She had three voice mails from Andrew, messages that she hadn't yet listened to. She closed her eyes, longing to hear the sound of his voice even if it was only in a voice mail.

She put down the phone. She had to be strong. He was already beginning to get his life back and she wouldn't drag him down with her again.

Her phone rang and she ignored it, fully expecting it to be Andrew. He would want her to know. He would want to share his good news with her. A tear slid down her face. She wanted to share it with him, but that wasn't possible and she couldn't give him false hopes by speaking to him.

She picked up the phone to turn it off, but noticed it wasn't Andrew calling. It was Mia.

She hit the answer button and heard Mia's frantic plea. "You have to help me, Jessica."

Her heart lurched. Had Mitch somehow gotten to Mia? "What's the matter? What's wrong?"

"I need you, Jessica. I have a friend who needs your help. She called me hysterical a few moments ago. I've been trying to convince her to leave her husband and tonight she escaped. She's alone, and I'm out of town. Can you help her?"

"Mia, I can't."

"I would normally just tell her to come to the shelter but I can't do that, can I? Please, Jessica, she's terrified. She needs someone to help her and I don't know who else to call."

Jessica stared at the clock. Agent Warren had said they were leaving in two hours. Surely that would be enough time to go and get this girl and take her somewhere safe. But her FBI bodyguards would never allow her to do that.

"Jessica, please!" The intensity in Mia's voice cracked through. The girl was afraid for her friend. This girl must be in real danger…and Jessica could never turn down someone in need.

"Where is she?"

She wrote down the address then promised Mia she would take care of her friend. But first she had to find a way to sneak past two FBI agents and, assuming she managed that, find a way to get there.

She thought about taking the shelter's van but the keys were up front. She would never make it past the agents if she tried to go get that key. Then she remembered the spare key in her desk drawer. She rummaged through until she found it.

Now to sneak outside without being spotted.

She slipped from her office and down the hallway toward the back door. She heard the agents moving around and talking from the common area. Fortunately for her, they were concerned with someone getting inside, not someone getting out.

She punched in the number to the alarm by the back door and it went offline. She opened the back door and crept quietly down the steps. She opened the gate and slipped out, moving quickly to the van.

She cautiously opened the driver's door and slid inside. She knew once she started the van, the agents would come to investigate. They would see the van missing but perhaps they would think it was a simple robbery. Perhaps they wouldn't immediately notice she was missing too.

She took a deep breath then turned the key in the ignition. She jolted the transmission into gear and took off before either of the agents inside could follow.

TWELVE

CJ seemed smug as she handed over the box of files on the Shroud case.

"I'm glad to be handing this one over to you," she told him. "This case just got even more complicated."

"How?"

"I spoke to a young woman a few days ago who claims Amy Vance had been threatening and harassing her. She's an old ex of Shroud's but says he wouldn't leave her alone. Then Amy got in on the harassment. Her testimony could tarnish the victim's reputation."

"We aren't putting the victim on trial, CJ." He skimmed through CJ's interview notes. "Amy was probably acting on behalf of Shroud." He thought back to the speech Jessica had given at the school. "It's called stalking by proxy. Typically, an assailant will have someone else, usually a new girlfriend, stalk and harass the victim."

He thought back to the classroom and the girl's discussion about how her boyfriend had asked her to place notes in another girl's locker.

He stopped as another thought hit him. How had Reynolds gotten so close to Jessica without someone noticing him? The FBI was acting on the assumption that someone was hiding him. Was it possible someone was helping him?

Someone close to Jessica?

He went over in his head all the events of the past few weeks. Jessica's stalker had been inside her house, in her yard, in her car, even at the shelter. Reynolds could never get that close on his own without someone noticing.

His mind played over the women in Jessica's life. Any one of those women was vulnerable to being used by Reynolds either through intimidation or charm.

Joan?

Danielle?

Amber?

Pamela?

Sarah?

He couldn't imagine she would be involved with Reynolds…but then he couldn't have imagined she would let Robert beat up on her, either.

Suddenly, the text from her to come to Dalton Lake clicked into place. Had she placed that text? Had she helped Reynolds set up her own brother?

He picked up his office phone and punched in his mother's telephone number. Sarah should have arrived there by now and he needed to hear the truth from her own lips.

She sounded bright and happy when she answered. Would she have left town if she was truly in cahoots with Reynolds?

"I have to ask you a question, Sarah, and I need you to answer me truthfully. It's important."

"Is something wrong, Andrew?"

"I'm not sure. I was looking over your statement about the night Robert died. Did…" Was he really going to accuse his sister of conspiring against him?

He sighed, resigned. He had to know the truth.

"Did you text me that day to meet you at Dalton Lake?"

He listened closely for signs that she was searching for what to say or for the right answer to give. But without hesitation, she denied it. "No. I didn't even have my phone."

"You left your phone?" He couldn't imagine his sister leaving without what she considered a vital piece of technology. "You always had that phone with you."

"I know but Mia took it from me that morning."

Mia?

"She caught me exchanging texts with Robert. She said I broke one of the rules of the shelter and she took my phone. She said she was going to tell Jessica, but when I didn't respond to him, Robert came over. You know the rest. I never got the phone back."

Mia!

Mia had the access to Jessica, to her house, her phone, even her office at the shelter.

Mia was the one helping Mitch Reynolds terrorize Jessica.

Jessica glanced at her watch. The woman was late. She hoped she hadn't had any trouble getting away. Jessica had no real idea what she was walking into but it couldn't be good given how frantic Mia had sounded.

Jessica still didn't know what she would do with this girl once she arrived safely. She'd already called all the shelters anywhere within driving distance and knew they were all full. Her mind searched for an alternative. Perhaps if she took the girl back to Dean's Den with her, the agents would help keep her safe.

She glanced up. Clouds darkened the sky and a light

drizzle began to fall. She started toward her car until she saw another car approaching. The headlights were on and glaring but she noticed the car slowed as it approached. This must be the woman she was waiting on.

The car turned into the lot. Jessica noticed it looked like Mia's sedan. The driver's-side door opened and a man got out, stopping Jessica in her tracks. She recognized the height and swagger of the man as he shut the door.

Mitch! This was a trap.

"Hello, Jess."

"What are you doing here? Where is Mia?"

He stepped toward her. "She served her purpose."

Jessica's heart plummeted. Had he killed Mia? She'd only spoken to her an hour ago. Jessica remembered the frantic tone of her voice and realized she'd sounded so upset because she'd been terrified.

"What do you want, Mitch? Why don't you just leave? You're out. You should be halfway across the country by now."

"I can't leave without you, Jess."

"You're not leaving with me."

He grinned in a smug, knowing way. "I've waited a long time for this moment, Jess. I'm not leaving."

Her only hope now was to escape. She turned and ran, heading for the van and jumping inside. Her fingers tried to grab for the keys but she struggled to find the right one then struggled to connect it with the ignition. The door opened and Mitch grabbed her arm, trying to pull her out. Jessica clung to the steering wheel but was no match for his strength. Her fingers loosened and he jerked her out the door. She fell against the pavement. She knew if she went with him she was dead. Her only hope was to run.

She rolled over to see him come at her, but a swift

kick to his knee sent him down. She kicked him again, this time connecting with his face then the shoulder she remembered had been shot.

Jessica jumped up, running as fast as she could into the brush, knowing he would be up and following her at any moment.

Andrew ran for his car, his only thought of getting to Jessica. He dialed her number again and again and each time it went straight to voice mail. He had to tell her what he figured out—Mia was the person helping Mitch Reynolds.

He left her a hasty message begging her to call him and warning her about Mia. Then he hung up and dialed Margo's number as he aimed his car toward the shelter.

"What's up, Andrew?" she said when she answered.

"I can't reach Jessica. It's Mia—Mia is the one helping Reynolds."

"Mia? How do you know?"

"She took Sarah's phone, the one that sent me the text message that lured me to the lake. She must have given it to Reynolds. Think about it, Margo, she would have had access to Jessica's house and her car. She could have been the one that planted the notes and flowers. She was with Jessica when Robert attacked. She would have known to run next door and get Reynolds. Plus, she would easily have been able to leave the back door and the gate unlocked for Reynolds to break in to the shelter."

He could hear realization dawn in her voice. "I can't believe it. Mia? How could she betray Jessica like that?" Then her voice simmered. "I'll kill her."

"I have to warn Jessica. I'm heading to the shelter right now."

"I'll update the agents and then get a warrant for Mia's apartment, phone and financial records."

He turned off State Street and noticed a commotion in the shelter's parking lot. "Something's wrong."

Six FBI vehicles sat in the lot and all the lights were on. Six agents were standing outside talking and several were rushing about.

"What's going on?" Margo demanded in his ear.

Andrew approached an agent yelling into his cell phone.

"Who are you?" the man demanded.

"My name is Andrew Jennings. I need to see Jessica Taylor."

The man scoped him out and he knew he was about to get the standard no-comment reaction.

"Who is that?" Margo demanded. "Is that Agent Robbins?"

The agent eyed Andrew's phone, obviously overhearing her voice through the speaker. "Is that Detective Stephens?" Andrew nodded then handed over the phone. "Margo, we have a problem. Jessica is gone. She sneaked out the back and took the van."

Agent Robbins held the phone out from his ear as Margo hollered at him through the phone.

Andrew stepped forward. "She wouldn't have left like that unless something happened. Mia must have called her, lured her out."

Agent Robbins nodded. "Lured her right into a trap."

Another agent came toward them. "Good news. The van has a GPS system. We were able to track it to Lookout Park at Dalton Lake."

Agent Robbins nodded. "Let's call the locals in to go looking for her. But warn them not to engage Reynolds. He's possibly armed and definitely dangerous."

He placed the phone back to his ear and addressed Margo. "Did you hear that? We're heading there now."

He pushed the phone back to Andrew and rushed toward a waiting SUV with Andrew fast on his heels.

Police lights were crammed into the parking lot at Lookout Park. Agent Robbins parked and jumped out and Andrew followed him. Robbins flashed his FBI identification and asked for the officer in charge.

"What have you found?" he asked when the officer responded.

He held up an evidence bag with a cell phone inside. "We found this on the ground just by the trees. Looks like she dropped it before running into those woods. There's some evidence that your guy followed her."

He spotted the van parked in the lot. A team of forensics officers were gearing up to examine it. "What's going on over there?"

"We found a possible blood sample on the ground beside the driver's seat." He pointed toward another car surrounded by cops. "But the real news is over here."

Andrew's heart stopped as he headed for the car. The trunk was wide-open and the crime scene staff was in full swing. This wasn't good. Something bad was inside that trunk. The rain pelted his face as each moment moved him closer and closer.

The officers parted as they approached and he spotted the bare skin of a knee. He could see it was a woman's. His heart stopped. Was it…?

He stepped closer and stared down into the trunk of the car. A woman's body was bound and gagged, her throat slashed.

Mia.

* * *

Jessica pushed through the brush. It bit at her legs and arms. Her muscles were jelly and her lungs ached from breathing. She couldn't go on much longer. She put her hands on her knees and fought to catch her breath.

Why hadn't she called someone before leaping into danger again?

Did anyone even know she was in trouble? Was anyone even looking for her?

She was alone. Totally alone.

Wasn't that what she'd wanted? Those she'd loved were safe from Mitch's grasp…but now who would come to her rescue?

She glanced around. Nothing was visible as far as she could see except woods. She should have come upon a clearing or a golf course or something by now. But then she was so turned around. She was unfamiliar with this area. For all she knew, she could be running in circles, or miles away from civilization.

Lost and alone.

Why hadn't she listened to Andrew's warning about lying low? Why hadn't she turned to the agents for help after Mia's call? Instead, she had plunged ahead, certain of her mission, prideful of her own importance.

She'd only wanted to help.

Now she was the one who needed it.

God, please help me.

She rested against a tree and closed her eyes. All around her, the sounds of nature whispered. The movements of the leaves as the wind blew, the sound of rain plopping against a puddle, the hums of the frogs and bugs surrounding her. A gentle reminder touched her soul. God had made all of this. He'd fashioned it with

His own hands. He knew every inch of these woods. He was not lost.

The verse where nature called His name came to her mind. She was not alone here. She felt His presence like never before. She had never been alone.

A louder sound pulled her from her reverie. It was greater than the calmness of the woods. It was an intruder in the midst.

Mitch!

She rose to her feet and listened as the movement grew closer, but she couldn't tell which way it was coming from. No way of knowing which way to run.

She tried to scream as someone clamped a hand over her mouth from behind. Panic burst through her.

He'd found her!

"It's me. It's Andrew."

Jessica spun around to face him. Relief flooded her face and she collapsed into his arms.

"What are you doing here?"

He touched her face, pushing away a tear that trickled down her cheek. "I told you I wouldn't let you face this alone."

She collapsed into his arms. Even after all she'd done to him, even after how she'd hurt him, Andrew had come for her. What had she done to deserve such love?

"Are you okay? Did he hurt you?" He scanned her for injuries. "If he harmed one hair on your head…"

"I'm okay…now that you're here."

"Jess!" Mitch's voice echoed through the scrub brush. "Where are you, Jess?"

Andrew took her hand. "We have to get out of here." He pulled her along behind him as he pushed through the scrub brush.

"How did you know where to find me?"

"Agent Warren tracked the GPS on the van. They're formulating a search of the woods looking for you and Mitch. I couldn't wait." He reached for his phone only to find the case empty. "I must have left my phone in the car. We're on our own for now. Let's head back toward the cabins. They'll be closed this time of year, but maybe someone is there who will have a way to call for help." He grabbed her hand and led the way. She followed, encouraged that Mitch would not be able to get to her.

God had sent her a hero.

They entered a clearing along the lake where rows of cabins sat on stilts. Down the way, he noticed the blue box indicating a pay phone. If he could get to that phone, he could let the police know exactly where they were.

He tugged at her hand and ran toward the phone, but the equipment was gone.

"What do we do now?"

"The FBI will have a search pattern. We stay alive until they find us." They ran toward one of the cabins, climbed the wooden steps and tried the door. It was locked so Andrew searched for something to break it open. He ran back down the steps and picked up a large rock from the flower garden surrounding the cabin and used it to break open the lock.

He ushered Jessica inside then used the rock to hold the door closed. It wouldn't keep Mitch out but perhaps it would buy them some time to hide out here.

"That door won't stop him," Jessica noted.

"First he has to find us." He held on to her and they slid to the floor, huddling together. She dug her face into his chest and cried.

"I'm sorry. This is all my fault. I shouldn't have run off

No Safe Haven

alone. I can hardly believe you came after me…especially after the awful things I said to you."

His embrace tightened. "I thought I'd lost you." His voice trembled as he processed the fear that he might never see her again. "I'm never leaving your side again."

"I'll hold you to that."

"Good." He stroked her cheek, his heart overflowing with love for her. She'd wriggled her way under his skin and stolen his heart. "You've changed my life, Jessica Taylor. You've become my life. I never knew I could love someone so irritating so much." He kissed her and she melted into his embrace.

Tears filled her eyes as she stared up at him. "Oh, Andrew, I lo—"

The sound of boots on the steps outside the door stopped her words.

Her eyes widened with fear. "It's him."

Mitch had found them.

Andrew pushed her behind him in a protective way. With each clomp on the wooden step, she gasped. Finally, Mitch seemed to have reached the top. Her fingers dug into Andrew's skin as the door knob rattled.

Andrew grabbed the iron poker by the fireplace then led Jessica toward the back of the cabin, taking refuge in one of the bedrooms. "The FBI aren't going to find us in time. You have to get out of here. Go to the window and jump. Don't stop running until you find help. I'll distract Mitch."

Jessica clung to him. "No, he'll kill you."

"It's you he wants. Run toward the main road. Don't look back no matter what. Don't let him find you, Jessica."

The crack of wood echoed through the cabin. Mitch was inside.

He opened the window and stared down. "It's a good drop."

She hugged him. "I'm afraid, Andrew."

"This ends now." Andrew kissed her then pushed her toward the window. "Go!"

She climbed up onto the sill and looked back at him, hesitating even as the sound of Mitch's boots against the wooden floor moved closer.

"Jessica, go!"

She jumped as the door burst open and Mitch rushed into the room, the gun in his hand aimed on Andrew.

"You've been a bad boy, Counselor, messing with someone else's girl."

He gripped the poker. "She is not your girl."

"She said she loved me."

"That was before she knew who you were...what you were."

"I'm willing to kill for her. Are you willing to die for her?"

Andrew lunged at him, swinging the poker with everything he had. He got several good blows before Mitch seized it and tossed it across the room. Andrew grabbed for the gun instead, trying to knock it from Mitch's grasp.

The gun discharged, sending white-hot pain ripping through Andrew's gut. His knees buckled and he fell to the floor gasping for breath. His head swam, threatening unconsciousness, but he couldn't let go. He couldn't let this maniac get to Jessica.

He grabbed for the poker again, forced his legs to stand and swung, connecting the iron rod to Mitch's skull. The big man fell to his hands and knees, the gun sliding out of reach as he fell. Andrew swung again and Mitch hit the floor, sprawling unconscious.

Andrew grabbed his stomach. Blood pooled on his

hand. He dropped the poker and slid to the floor as the darkness descended.

At least Jessica was safe.

Pain ripped through Jessica's knee as she hit the ground. The crack of the door breaking open echoed through the window as did Mitch's and Andrew's voices.

Jessica took off running, gasping with pain with each step.

The sound of a gunshot stopped her in her tracks. She jumped behind a tree and peered back toward the cabin, waiting to see which man emerged.

Please, God, let it be Andrew.

Several minutes of anguish passed before she heard movement in the cabin. Mitch emerged from the door, scanned the area then stumbled down the steps, unsteady on his feet and clutching his head.

She leaned against the tree for support. Hot tears scalded her eyes. Mitch had left the cabin alone, but where was Andrew? Was he hurt? Was he dead?

She had to know.

Mitch shook his head to clear it and swore as he mopped blood from his face. But he moved on toward the other cabins, obviously still searching for her.

When he was out of sight, Jessica cautiously made her way back toward the cabin. She ignored the pain in her knee as she limped up the steps and stumbled inside toward the back room.

She fell to the floor when she saw Andrew and crawled to his side where he lay. Blood pooled around him and his face was pale and cold.

Andrew couldn't die. He couldn't die.

Hot tears rained down on his face as she held him.

It seemed time had stopped and rewound, only this

time it was Andrew instead of Dean lying in a pool of blood. Her worst nightmare was being replayed, no matter how hard she'd tried to stop it.

She heard Mitch's boots on the steps again. This time instead of blind fear, it was fury that spread through her.

She saw the gun on the floor by the fireplace and reached for it. It was heavy and cold in her hand, but she lifted it and aimed it at the door, right at Mitch's head as he entered. But, despite her bravado, her hand shook as she held it.

He laughed when he saw it. "Well, well, we're right back here again, aren't we?"

She flashed back to that awful night Dean had died. She'd held a gun on Mitch then too, but she hadn't been able to pull the trigger and Dean had lost his life because of her failure.

She clutched the gun with both hands. "I will shoot you, Mitch."

"We both know you won't shoot me, Jess."

Fire surged through her at the familiarity of the nickname. He had no right to pretend they were on intimate terms. She'd practiced for this day for years. She'd imagined his face on every target. But now, with him standing in front of her, she realized she hadn't accounted for the fear. Mitch terrified her because she knew what he was capable of.

He toyed with her, taunting her, circling. She followed him, the gun remaining on him. She wouldn't let him out of this one, but her nerve failed her. She couldn't will her fingers to pull the trigger.

"You don't threaten me, Jess. You're weak. You always were. That's what got Dean killed. That's why I had to kill Andrew. It's your fault."

She shook her head at his accusations. Hadn't she believed the same thing all this time?

"No!"

She wouldn't believe his lies, not this time.

He laughed. "There's that fire I love."

Her skin crawled at his intimate manner. "You don't know what love is, Mitch. You never have. You don't love me. You're obsessed with me. And it has nothing to do with me. It's all about you. You like the control you have over me."

"And you think you know all about love? I guess you think that A.D.A. loves you?"

"I know he does, and I love him. But I'm talking about the love of Jesus Christ." Dean had died because he loved her. Andrew might be dead because he loved her, but Jesus had been the first to die for her, the first to love her so much that He gave His life for her.

She clutched the gun in her hand and prayed for the strength of God to empower her. It was the only thing that would get her through this.

Mitch snarled and moved toward her again. She pulled the trigger, jolting at the recoil that nearly knocked her off her feet. She recovered quickly and fired again and again until Mitch fell to the floor and didn't get back up.

She let the gun slip from her hand. Tears fell from her eyes and she didn't hold them back. It was over. Finally, it was over. But at what cost?

The thud of helicopter blades told her the police had finally found them. She heard footsteps on the stairs then movement at the door. Margo and Agent Robbins entered, guns pulled and ready for action, followed by a squad of men with guns and vests.

Margo rushed to her and threw her arms around Jessica. "Don't scare me like that again."

Agent Robbins moved toward Mitch and checked for a pulse. "He's dead." He eyed the gun at her feet. "You did this?" At her nod, he responded, "Good job."

Margo pulled off her jacket and draped it across Jessica. "Let's get you out of here."

"Andrew!" She turned to where Andrew lay still unmoving. A team of EMTs hovered over him, working fervently.

"Let the paramedics tend to him."

But Jessica knew it was too late. She'd seen his face and felt the cold clamminess of his skin.

Just as it had with Dean, help had come too late to save Andrew.

THIRTEEN

The emergency room was bustling with activity while Jessica sat in the hard plastic seats of the waiting room. A few feet away, Margo and Agent Robbins were engaged in a heated, whispering debate and every now and then their voices would rise and they would glance her way.

Finally, Margo walked away, poured a cup of coffee and sat down beside Jessica.

"What's going on there?" Jessica asked her, motioning toward Agent Robbins, whose folded arms and firm expression indicated he wasn't happy with the outcome of their discussion.

"He needs to take your statement. I told him he had to wait until we got news about Andrew."

Jessica shook her head as she thought of all that had been lost because of Mitch. "So many people are dead because of him. Mia—"

"Who conspired against you with him." The bitterness in Margo's voice caught Jessica off guard.

"She was a young innocent girl who Mitch used and then killed. She was as much a victim of him as I was."

"Well, you're more forgiving than I am."

"Mitch hurt a lot of people. Mrs. Brady, Mr. Percy."

Margo stopped her. "Actually, I have news about Mr. Percy."

"You found his body?"

"Sort of. Apparently he met a hot young widow at the VA luncheon and they decided to fly to Vegas and get married."

"You mean Mr. Percy is alive?"

"Alive, and a newlywed."

Jessica hardly had time to be thankful for that news when the door opened and a man in scrubs headed their way. "I'm Dr. Studdard. Are you with Mr. Jennings?"

"Yes." Jessica stood to greet him, half afraid to hear what he had to say, but anxious just to know. She searched his face for any clues but the man was obviously skilled at keeping his expression blank.

Please, Lord, let Andrew be all right.

But then she remembered the way he'd looked, the way his skin had felt when she'd touched him.

She braced herself for bad news.

"He lost a lot of blood, but we were able to remove the bullet and repair the damage to his abdomen. We also had to reset a broken bone in his left arm, but overall he was fortunate. He's going to be just fine."

Margo squealed and hugged her, but Jessica was unable to copy her outwardly enthusiastic expression. A flood of thankfulness washed through her. God was so good. He'd not only given her back her life, He'd given her a man to share it with. Suddenly, those visions of family and happily ever after didn't seem so far-fetched.

"Can I see him?" Jessica asked.

The doctor led them into a room where Andrew was lying on the bed. He still wasn't moving, but the monitors he was hooked to indicated his blood pressure and heart rate were fine. She moved a chair up beside the bed and held his hand, thankful that the color and warmth had returned to his skin.

She closed her eyes and said a prayer of thanks for all that the Lord had given her but mostly for the hope He'd restored.

Andrew opened his eyes to a blurry scene. A television mounted on the wall, a closed curtain and monitors. His foggy mind tried to focus. He was in a hospital room. He tried to move and pain seared through his shoulder. He looked down and saw the bandage. His arm was in a cast.

Memories came floating back to him. He'd been shot. Mitch had shot him.

Suddenly, he was wide-awake with worry. Jessica! Where was Jessica?

"Andrew, I'm here."

He felt her hand take his and a warm, calming sensation flowed through him. She'd had that effect on him ever since the start. He raised his head and saw her sitting beside the bed. He tightened his grip on her hand then pulled it up to his lips.

"I thought I'd lost you there for a minute."

She smiled a smile that brightened up the room. "That was supposed to be my line. You were the one who got shot." She stroked his cheek. "How do you feel?"

How did he feel? As if he'd been lost and was now found. As if the world was right again as long as she was by his side. Gratitude rushed through him. God had truly given him the desires of his heart. "I'm better now."

She caressed his temple, pushing back his hair. "You don't have to be brave. I know you're in pain. You don't have to be strong all alone anymore."

He squeezed her hand. "I'm not alone." And he never

had been, he realized. God had always been with him. "What about Reynolds? Did they capture him?"

"We don't have to worry about him anymore. He can't hurt us ever again."

Was it possible they were free of this albatross of fear and pain? Finally free to make a life together? He longed to shout to the world all that God had restored to him.

He sat back in the bed, his memory of events slowly returning. He remembered struggling with Mitch and the gun going off. But one moment of the afternoon stood out in his memory. "When we were in the cabin…when I told you I loved you…you were about to say something in return." He glanced in her eyes. "Something important?"

She leaned over and kissed his cheek, whispering her response into his ear. "I was going to say I love you. I do love you, Andrew. I'm sorry I didn't tell you sooner. I'm sorry I tried to push you away. I only wanted to protect you, but you risked your life to come after me. You wouldn't let me go."

His heart soared that she was able to speak those words without fear or regret. "Never, Jessica. I'll never let you go."

"Do you know how many times I've heard those words said with evil intent behind them? How many times those words have sent terror ripping through me?"

"But not this time?"

"No, Andrew, because this time, they're coming from you."

* * * * *

Dear Reader,

Thank you for reading Andrew and Jessica's story. I am so thrilled that theirs has become my first published LIS because I feel such a connection with these characters. We all have a past. We've all been hurt either by our own choices or by the choices of those around us. We have all gone through something in our pasts, and this world in which we live teaches us many different ways to cope. However, as Andrew and Jessica's story shows, true healing comes only through the power of Jesus Christ. And according to 2 Samuel 14:14, God devises ways to bring His children back to Him. Isn't that awesome? We serve a God who actively works to restore us to Himself no matter how many wrong choices we've made or wrong roads we've traveled.

One of my favorite verses is Joel 2:24 that states God will restore what the locusts ate. God restored Jessica from a traumatic experience. He gave her life a passion to help other abused women as well as a second chance at love. In a similar way, God has restored my life from the wrong choices I made in my younger days. He has given me a heart for women's ministry and a passion for encouraging women to understand why we make the choices we make.

I would love to hear your thoughts, comments or stories of restoration. You can visit my website at virginiavaughanonline.com, my blog at womenofconsequence.blogspot.com, or through the publisher.

Blessings!
Virginia

Questions for Discussion

1. Jessica's passion to help abused women stems from her own past abuse. How can God use your past hurts to help others in similar situations?

2. In the beginning, Andrew equates success with courtroom wins and getting his face on the nightly news. By the end of the story, he shuns media attention and has a new understanding of justice. How did his journey change his perspective?

3. Jessica feels responsible for her brother's death because of her involvement with Mitch. Have you ever been involved in something that caused harm to someone you loved? If so, how did you feel afterward?

4. Andrew is at first very frustrated with his sister's behavior and doesn't understand why he can't help her. He wants to be the protective big brother but is unable to change her situation on his own. Do you have relatives or friends whose behavior baffles you? How do you cope with their wrong choices and your inability to change their ways?

5. Jessica teaches Andrew that even strong people can be victimized. How does this revelation help him to become a better prosecutor?

6. Even after all she has witnessed working with Jessica, Mia is still fooled by the handsome face and charm of Mitch. What factors might have led her

to become manipulated by Mitch? In the beginning, Andrew believed Jessica enjoyed the thrill of the risks she took. He discovers these risks have a greater purpose. Have you ever looked at a situation and judged a person's actions based on a past experience? How could you be misjudging that person?

7. Jessica believes that keeping her past a secret from even her closest friends makes her strong. How does this secret actually hinder her in her work? How does the truth coming out actually make her a stronger woman?

8. After Tory's death, Andrew pulled away from his faith and his friends in order to keep from dealing with his emotions. How do you handle difficult situations when they arise? Do you hide from difficult emotions? Or do you find comfort in fellow believers?

9. Jessica's brother died protecting her. When she realizes Mitch has returned, she tries to push Andrew away, fearful that he too will die trying to protect her. Have you ever tried to protect someone from the consequences of your wrong choices? How did that work out for you?

10. After her experience with Mitch, Jessica questions her ability to make good judgments where men are concerned. How important is it to have friends and family that will be honest with you about the choices you are making?

11. Andrew and Jessica both believe they can deal with

their past hurts without help, but they both only make their lives more difficult. It is only when they each allow someone else to share their burden, and finally give it over to Jesus, that they experience true healing. What pain in your life are you holding back from sharing with others?